In *The Lost of Syros,* a debut collection of stories by Emma Timpany, revelations come unexpectedly: in a shower of gold on a snow-covered volcano in Antarctica; at a graffiti-scarred Aboriginal sacred site; in a mouthful of cake. Precise and delicately written, these stories are little windows into life.

Emma Timpany was born and grew up in Dunedin, New Zealand. Her stories have won awards including The Sara Park Memorial Short Story Award 2013, The Society of Authors' Tom-Gallon Trust Award 2011 and The Society of Women Writers and Journalists' Short Story Award 2011. A pamphlet of her stories, *Over The Dam,* was published by Red Squirrel Press in April 2015. She currently lives in Cornwall.

www.emmatimpany.wordpress.com

'The Glasshouse Mountains' is a potent mix of three things: first, some fabulous writing; second, an intriguing theme explored in an original way; and third, that most elusive of things – that indefinable quality which gets under the skin of a readers' memory, and won't quite let you forget it.

Vanessa Gebbie
Judge of The Society of Women Writers and
Journalists' Short Story Award 2011

[The Pledge is] a finely tuned story about the instinct for love and duty.
Jane Gardam and Jacob Ross
Judges of the Tom-Gallon Award 2011

These poignant stories are so skilfully constructed they draw you effortlessly into different times and places. Precise, yet delicately written, they are little windows into life, showing you things to think on long after you have finished reading them. This is a superb debut collection that will resonate with me for a long time to come.

Rupert Wallis
Author of *The Dark Inside*

For Adam, Iris and Lauren, with all my love

The Lost
of Syros

Emma Timpany

Other books by the author

Over The Dam Red Squirrel Press (2015)

The Lost
of Syros

Emma Timpany

Cultured Llama Publishing

First published in 2015 by
Cultured Llama Publishing
11 London Road
Teynham, Sittingbourne
ME9 9QW
www.culturedllama.co.uk

ISBN 978-0-9932119-2-8

Printed in Great Britain by Lightning Source UK Ltd

Cover image from an original painting by Adam Drouet

Cover design by Mark Holihan

Contents

The Glasshouse Mountains

From a distance, the mountains appeared to be coloured pale rose, moss green – if the light was right you might even say a glimmering ice blue – as they rose above the plain. In the surrounding fields, pineapples pushed pink and green striped leaves out of the hot, red earth. Mike steered the campervan down the black roads of the coastal hinterland, over the bodies of cane toads squashed into the melting tarmac, past stands of thin trees, flaky with dust. Roads seemed to approach the mountains before suddenly veering away. The yellow and black AA signs helped little.

'That looks like a parking place there.'

Amy pointed, turning the map again in her hands, and Mike pulled in, over the gum-nut strewn ground and parked near a faded green Holden. A young man sat on the bonnet, watching them. When they turned off the engine, he pulled a bong from the passenger seat and lit it. Amy thought she could hear it bubbling, beneath the whirr of the fan trying to cool the engine. With the air-con off, Amy felt sweat prickle her skin. A flock of lorikeets screamed past, loud as a gang of teenage girls on their way to a party.

'Is this it?'

Mike pushed his fringe back from his forehead. When Mike sweated, he didn't go red, like she did; his clothing became soaked, as if by an internal rainstorm. Amy peered up at the mountain – which one was it? There was no sign, but it must be one of the little ones, maybe Ngungun or Miketeebumulgrai? They had looked so pretty from further away but now, close up, the mountain seemed brown and dreary. She tried not to look at the man outside.

'There's a girl with a baby in the back of the car,' Mike whispered.

'Don't stare.' Amy felt her teeth clench. 'Do you want to stay? Maybe we should go?'

'We might as well take a look, now we're here.'

Did Mike feel that tingle of fear as she did, stepping out of the camper under the gaze of the man? Around them, wind stirred the gum leaves so they chattered like teeth.

'G'day,' the man said and she replied, 'Oh, hi.'

There *was* a girl in the back, not much more than a teenager, with one of those cheap, imported gypsy-style skirts on; she was a small, dark-haired thing, with a heart-shaped face. A baby was suction-cupped to her breast.

'Shane,' the girl said, in a hard whisper, 'get in the car.'

Shane ignored her. 'You going up there?'

Mike retied the laces of his plimsolls. 'Yeah.'

Shane raised his eyebrows, as if human motivation were unfathomable, before relighting the bong. The sweet, sticky smell of marijuana filled the air, and the shrieks of the lorikeets seemed even louder. Amy felt a smile fix on her face, the sort of smile that came when she was uncertain, or afraid. As they walked away, she thought she could feel Shane watching them. They found a rough path and, beyond a stand of prickly bush, steps cut into the rock, edged with boards.

'He's going to break into the van and nick our stuff, isn't he?'

'Have you got the money belt? We're insured, aren't we?'

'Yeah, I just hate the thought of it.'

'I suggested we go. You're the one that wanted to have a look around.'

'Yeah, but I didn't realise Mr Bong Head would be lurking nearby.'

Hadn't he? Hadn't they both seen the same things as they pulled into the parking space? Her favourite defence was flight; given the slightest excuse, she would throw over whatever plans she'd made and change tack, zigzagging in a probably futile attempt to outrun her fate. Mike's logic and organisation grounded her; he was her antidote against the recurring venom of her snakebite of a childhood.

Silence fell, and by some sort of telepathic, mutual consent, they began to climb. Someone had sprayed religious graffiti on every other step. One of the slogans – *Kill Desire* – had been given an extra é and turned into *Kill Desireé*. There was graffiti on the rock itself, too, but it was more prosaic, the usual f-words and c-words, all correctly spelt, she noticed. She imagined the local boys from Beerwah and Mooloolaba cruising up here, late at night, with their cans of Four X and their spray paint. Did they ever cross paths with the Jesus freak? *Jesus is your shield* – he almost made it easy for them to change the final *d* to an *a* – as if they were playing an elaborate game of graffiti tag.

Halfway up the mountain was a cave.

'Wanna go in?' Mike asked.

'Nah.' There would probably be needles and spray cans and human waste. Remembering something she'd read in the guide book, she said, 'Lots of First World War soldiers settled here in the 1930s. To farm pineapples.'

'Strange,' Mike said. 'Why pineapples, I wonder?'

'It didn't work out – I don't know why – so they planted pine trees instead.'

'Pineapples. Pine trees. I see a pattern emerging. What's next, I wonder?' He paused, wiping sweat from his stubble. 'Pine nuts, surely.' He stabbed his finger in triumph.

The humidity wrapped round her, making her feel as if she were tangled in vast, warm, wet sheets. Creeklets of sweat ran down the backs of Mike's calves and he swotted at them, mistaking them for the ticklish dance of flies. She fought the urge to turn and run back to the campervan, back home to London, anywhere so long as it was away from here – there was something leaden in the air, despite the brightness of the scorching sun.

'Shall we go on?'

'Is it far, do you think?' Her life was made up of things she hadn't done because she'd been too busy zigzagging, trying to shake the past off her tail. Most of the living she'd done was because of Mike, through him – even if it wasn't *exactly* what she *wanted* to be doing, at least she was doing *something*. 'On we go,' she said.

The path got narrower as they climbed. Around them, eucalypts sighed, as if bored to death. She hadn't noticed a single lizard, although there were plenty of flies, now enjoying a pool party on Mike. His tee shirt and hatband were stained with sweat. They'd have to find somewhere to wash tonight – a campsite with facilities, or a clean stretch of beach, away from the muddy outlets of rivers, where unseen dangers lurked. She shuddered, feeling half a corpse already, as a fly tried to settle in the corner of her mouth.

Why had she brought Mike here? Was it because, though she'd never lived here, she was half-Australian? She used to come in the school holidays and stay with relatives in Brisbane; they'd often drive past this stretch of coast on the way to Noosa. That childhood gazing out of car windows, looking towards these mountains, coloured like things from a dream, had called her back fourteen years later, Mike in tow – it was a way of explaining her past to him. Her relatives had never brought her here – they knew this place was wrong – that's why they'd sped past again and again, to huddle in the next strip of restaurants and shops, only leaving the pavements to settle on the cleanest, most manicured strip of beach.

During those holidays she'd spent most of her time in the air-conditioned shopping malls of Brisbane. Halfway up this mountain, they struck her with an appeal she'd never felt before. She'd moaned to Mike that she'd been dumped there with twenty dollars to last her the day and that anything could have happened to her, but now it seemed much safer than this; the syringe-littered caves, the graffiti and Shane with the bong who was no doubt breaking into their campervan right about now.

'Mike, wait.' Breathing in this hot air made her faint. What would he think if she dragged him off to spend the rest of the week in Chermside or Indooroopilly? If together they roamed, not the rainforest, but the aisles of Myers, K-Mart and Target?

'We're here.'

The path spread open, and they walked out onto a high, open space; an almost flat platform ringed by rocky knobbles. Between the rocks lay hollows filled with dead-looking dirt. There was an explosion of graffiti near the last of the steps, but up here the artists seemed to have lost their verve, as if only the close confines of the climb inspired them. When she looked back at it, some of the metallic paint had the abstract, glistening quality of those Aboriginal paintings made up of lots of small dots – at dusk, it must shimmer almost magically. But, she remembered, there was no real dusk here, so close to the Equator, just a brief, cocktail-gaudy sunset before night fell.

5

'Well,' said Mike, 'that's a view.'

They looked out over pines and eucalypts, fields of pineapple and tobacco, the bluish sheen of avocado trees. The word 'beloved' came into her mind – this landscape had once been loved, but the people who had loved it had fled; without them, it didn't work – they had gone north, or to the red centre, to the places without roads and fields slicing everything up; they'd gone back to the places where the past was beside you, in the forgotten moment two heartbeats before this one.

'The Glasshouse Mountains are twenty million year old volcanic cones.' Mike read from the guidebook. 'Eroded to rock cores.'

The blink of an eye, Amy thought; if only that dead-looking dirt were time she would pick a handful of it up and sprinkle it over these rocks, peel back the roads like liquorice straps and cast them into the sea, knock over fences and sweep the newcomers down and away, back to Sydney and on to their ships, until the native forests grew again. Sighing, she reached for Mike's hand.

'What are you thinking about?' Mike kissed her cheek.

'Oh,' she said, 'all sorts of things.'

'Funny place, isn't it?'

'It's not what I expected.'

'Me neither.'

'But I'm glad we came.'

Up there, high and god-like, she thought of the white interior of the Queen Street mall: the cool tiles, the fluorescent lights, the sparkle of cheap silver offering something it couldn't deliver. As they made their way down, the religious graffiti was invisible, hidden beneath the steps. Passing the empty mouth of the cave, she thought of the artefacts her culture would leave behind there, and what might have been left there before; an unwanted infant or perhaps an elder, too sick or frail to move. As they neared the bottom of the track, they heard lorikeets gossiping

6

amongst a stand of paw-paws; a green globe fell on the ground, splitting open to show pumpkin-yellow flesh and a heart made of black seeds.

Back at the campervan, the other car had gone. Their van was untouched.

'Probably took one look at us and realised there was nothing worth nicking.' Mike swept his hand over his faded tee shirt, his shabby shorts. 'Ready for some lunch?'

It was too hot for lunch. They climbed back in the van and locked the doors. Mike started the engine and the air-conditioning came on. She picked up the guidebook to see whether they could find somewhere nearby to eat and look back at the mountain in safety, from behind a wall of glass.

A Walk in the Forest

Everyone said they were lucky with the weather. It was a fine, clear day, unusual in a part of the country notorious for its very high rainfall; temperate rainforest clothed the mountains, stretching from the shores of the lake all the way to the West Coast.

It was a long time since Sarah had been home, and an even longer time since she had walked in the forest. You could enter the track by a bridge across the dam at the foot of the lake, as she and the child did; otherwise there was another entry point a few kilometres downstream where a swing bridge straddled the wide, green-grey river. It only took a very short time, three or four minutes from either entrance, until you crossed the water and entered the trees. In both directions, for long stretches, the path through the forest was almost flat, a rich springy surface of decaying beech leaves; beyond it were moss-covered humps and mounds and stumps and the occasional hole, bare-earthed as a grave, where the root ball of a tree, now fallen, had once stood.

As the trees enclosed them – small-leaved southern beech, the fir-like podocarps, the smaller glossy-leaved coprosmias and manukas, black-stemmed with sooty mould – the child, letting go of Sarah's hand, ran ahead before stopping to peer and prod at patches of pale grey lichen, filmy ferns and some strange moss which rose from the ground on a slender stem before dividing into two wing-shaped halves as if it may, at any moment, rise and fly away.

If things had not changed so totally, Sarah and the child would not be in the forest but on the other side of the mountains, in their rain shadow, where the hillsides were dry and desert-like, coated in golden tussock grass and studded, at this time of year, with yellow-leaved poplars, a purple-blue haze of viper's bugloss, the glossy red hips of wild dog roses. The child, after looking again at the trees and placing an exploratory foot in a hole, with a quick glance over her shoulder towards her mother, said, 'Come on, Creamy,' and mounting her imaginary horse, cantered ahead until, rounding a bend in the path, she was lost from sight.

For a moment there was only silence, a great gush of it, and the deep, soothing green presence of the trees all around until a cold buzz of fright in Sarah's veins told her to hurry after the child. She found her a little further on, standing under the green umbrella of a tree fern, examining a ghost-pale clump of coral moss. Sarah knew what it felt like, that moss – it was cool and light, spongy, as if it belonged in the sea – because she had come to this forest, or one very like it, many years ago on a school trip. Back then, the teacher had shown them little stands of orchids growing on fallen logs.

In Sarah's memory, the orchids were sometimes green, sometimes white, and she remembered the teacher telling them how lucky they were to see them. Had it been because the orchids were rare, or because they were difficult to spot? What were plants called that fed on others? Despite their beauty, were they parasites? She had not liked that teacher much partly because of his strange appearance; he was as lipless as the mantis shrimps they had captured on the sand flats of Otakau at low tide. Sarah remembered how desperately the shrimps had dived as, armed with spades, they dug them up, before transporting them back to the classroom aquarium where each day she had watched them bury themselves again and again in their tank of sand.

She had been older then than the child was now; just beginning to understand the undertows and rips of her family, still fighting, not yet dragged far out from shore and drowned. But the peacefulness of the trees, the great greenness of them, seemed somehow to subdue even that painful history. It perhaps had something to do with the lack of noise, litter, colour in this place; there was no horizon to aim for, only an occasional glimpse of sky; she had no greater ambition than to take another step along the brown path which wound through the green, though at times a tree grew right in its middle, splitting its flow as an island divides a river.

The child did not know what had happened, would not know until she was older, perhaps the same age as Sarah had been when she had first come to the forest and not long after, at the insistence of her mother, given up her share of her father's estate. The talk at the time had been of fairness but, as everyone except Sarah had known, life is not fair; it was true, also, that Sarah had been unlucky, that those who should have protected her, advised her, had her best interests at heart, hadn't: she had not been able to look into the future; how could she have guessed what would happen? Now it was all gone; it would never again be hers; it would never be the child's.

What is still mine?, she wanted to ask the trees. *Now I*

have lost so much, are you still mine?

'We should go back.' The memories brought her feet to a stop, heart pounding as if they had strayed dreamily, like two innocents in a fairy story, off the path, or turned to see the birds had eaten the trail of crumbs they had dropped, and they were lost, lost.

'Not yet, Mummy. Please.'

It was all right. The path was there, black-brown and soft beneath her feet. The trees had not swallowed them. And who knew when they might be able to come back here again?

'Okay, we'll go on, but just a little further.'

Sarah had expected the child to be tired, to moan about sore legs and aching feet. But the leaves were pleasant to walk on, and there was something about the trees, something about how they were so similar and yet so different, so obviously a family and yet separate that she could not have explained but which soothed her, or perhaps it was simply walking down the curving path, surrounded by bird calls, mounds of milk moss, swaying curtains of old man's beard hanging from branches, the sudden exposed earth of the holes and all the time the child quietly singing and at times the gentle sound of the river or the lapping of waves against an unseen shore as boats passed far out in the green-black vastness of the lake.

When the path wound down a gully through a crowd of tree ferns, they followed it.

'Mum, come and see, come and see.'

The child, who had been bending over a fallen log, stood back. The roots grew on the outside of the trunk, and the leaves were strong and glossy, the flowers white with pale yellow centres, tiny yet exquisite; above the dying wood, hundreds of stems of snow-white orchids quivered. Soft, luminous, white, waxy petals; sweet-smelling yellow mouths turned up towards her as if they were hungry. Sarah had begun a BSc, majoring in Botany, but had left university halfway through her second year; she had had to get away, had gone overseas; her life, until the child had been born, had unfolded in a city where she had sometimes walked the streets on summer nights reciting the names of the plants that grew, sooty and neglected, in other people's front gardens. But now, back in the forest, the things she had learned at school and her brief time at university came back to her: the white orchid was not a parasite but an epiphyte, a plant which though it grows on another does not take anything from it.

It was a long time before Sarah said anything. The child seemed content looking at the flowers before turning and solemnly addressing the empty air beside her to tell Creamy not to eat them in case they were 'poison'.

'We're lucky. Lucky.' The words seemed to release a weight from Sarah's chest, as if, without realising it, she'd been holding her breath.

'Yes,' said the child.

Gathering up invisible reins, the child remounted Creamy and began to gallop ahead. There was still some way to go. Sarah had been thinking that at some point they would have to turn back and retrace their steps to the dam, but surely it would be just as easy to carry on and exit by the swing bridge; they could catch one of the regular buses back to the village. If the child grew very tired, Sarah would carry her.

The Pledge

Toby hurried in the front door, loaded down with plastic bags. Outside, the rain was torrential. 'Ginny? Seb? You home?' Water dripped from the end of Toby's nose onto his chin. As he moved forward, his sodden shoes squelched. He dropped the grocery bags on the mat, shrugged off his backpack and coat. 'Ginny?'

No reply, but the sound of some grunge band started up so she was in residence, at least. Toby kicked his shoes off. He pushed open the living room door – there was Seb, cross-legged on the sofa, staring at the TV screen. An aura of light from the television spilled towards him, seeming to reach for him like some blue, inhuman caress.

'Why don't you put the light on, Seb?' As Toby scolded him he reminded himself that all thirteen-year-olds were exasperating. Seb had a kind, gentle nature; he might be messy and inconsiderate but he wasn't cruel. He wished he could say the same about Ginny, who was fifteen and more out of control every day.

Toby crossed the room, pausing to straighten the Persian rug before pulling the curtains together. When he looked back, Seb had his eyes half-closed, his thumb slotted into his mouth. Wind-driven rain hit the glass and made the sash window rattle. Toby shivered as he felt a draught creep in under the curtain. Re-crossing the room, he stopped to ruffle Seb's hair.

'I'll get the dinner on – bet you're starving, eh?' He remembered the constant hunger he'd felt at thirteen.

Toby carried the bags into the kitchen, his toes recoiling against the cold of the slate floor tiles. Bloody Ginny; she'd made cheese on toast and left a tide-line of cheese and crumbs and Worcester sauce across the work surface. She knew how carefully he cleaned up after breakfast. Every afternoon before he got home she'd mess things up. He felt like stomping up there and shaking her skinny shoulders, but he wouldn't, of course, and she knew it.

He pulled some old tartan fur-lined slippers out of the shoe rack, flicked on the heating and made himself a cup of coffee. Five thirty. He chopped onions, crying the whole time and rubbing onion juice in his eyes as he tried to wipe the tears away.

'You crying, Dad?' Seb had come in to the kitchen. 'When's tea ready?'

'It'll be an hour. Why don't you do some homework?'

'Haven't got any.'

Toby raised his eyebrows; Seb picked up his schoolbag and started decanting books onto the kitchen table. 'And Seb…?'

'Yeah?'

'Don't call me Dad.'

'Okay.' Seb paused. 'But what do you expect, wearing those slippers?'

Toby growled and threw a tea towel at Seb.

Seb said, 'Ow,' but playfully. He folded the towel into an Arab-style headdress, which he plonked on his scruffy hair, and then began scribbling in a notebook.

Toby fried mince, added sliced mushrooms, peppers, courgettes. He took a sip of coffee and spluttered – too hot; it burnt his tongue. It was turning out to be one of those days, or, to be precise, another one of those days. He opened the can of chopped tomatoes with extreme caution – the way things were going he'd no doubt slice his finger on the lid. Soon the sauce was bubbling away. He added a final spoonful of olives and a sprinkling of herbs.

'Smells good.'

'I'm just going to get changed out of my uniform. When I come down I'll put the pasta on.'

Seb seemed engrossed in doing his homework; that was one less battle to fight, at least. Toby climbed the stairs to his bedroom, undressed and laid his uniform with care over the arm of a cane chair. He'd have to wait for his trousers to dry and brush the cuffs in the morning when they were no longer wet. Wet – that reminded him, Seb's bed had needed changing again this morning. He'd stripped the sheets and put them in the machine first thing while he'd been making the breakfast and packed lunches. He'd remembered to hang the sheets out on the line before running to catch the bus. But the rain – there'd be no getting them dry tonight. Toby sighed, pulling on a sweatshirt and jeans, then stripped the sheets from his bed and used them to make up Seb's. When that was done, he sat for a moment on the edge of the bed and placed his head in his hands.

'What are you doing in Seb's room?'

Ginny stood in the doorway. She'd dyed her hair pink.

'I'm...nothing.' Don't react; it'll only make things worse. Count to three (one, elephant, two, elephant, three, elephant) then take a deep breath.

'Did Seb wet the bed again last night?'

Toby nodded. Ginny blinked. He noticed her eyes were bloodshot. She kicked at a pile of dirty clothes, which lay slumped against the wardrobe.

'Is dinner ready?'

'Yep. I just need to put on the pasta and grate some cheese.' If there was any cheese left, after she'd spread it all over the kitchen. 'Oh, and Ginny…'

'Yeah?'

He looked at her pink hair, her red-rimmed eyes. 'Never mind.'

'This is delicious, Dad.' Seb gulped forkfuls of pasta and sauce. 'Is there any more?'

'Plenty, but have some salad, too.'

Seb made those big, pleading 'do I have to?' eyes at him and Toby smiled.

'Thanks, Dad.'

'For God's sake will you stop calling him that?' Ginny had eaten her small bowlful quickly and now sat, arms folded, scowling at them. Her pink hair was spiked with gel, a rosy crown of thorns. Last week her hair had been long and blond, the week before that, black.

'I can call him what I want.'

'Can't even stop pissing yourself, can you, weirdo?'

'Ginny, Seb, please…'

'He started it!'

'You did!' Seb said then muttered, 'Freak.'

Toby stood and walked over to the phone. He picked up the receiver. 'Do you want me to ring…?'

'No!' They both shouted.

'…because I will, I swear to God, unless you two stop it. I can't take it, okay? Do you hear me?' A silence, which he hoped was filled with resolutions for better behaviour, followed. 'Okay, now – dessert?'

'What is there?'

'Ice cream and berries.'

'I'll do it.' She stood and collected their plates.

Despite the hair, despite the hardness, Ginny looked

closer to twelve than fifteen. At least this week she was eating; sometimes she went for days without, and it frightened him.

'Thanks, Ginny.'

'Thanks, Ginnster.'

They ate dessert in silence, apart from the scrape of spoon on bowl, which set his teeth on edge. When they finished, Ginny said, 'I'm going to have a bath; this colour washes out.'

'Then homework, okay?'

She nodded and went upstairs. Toby heard water gushing from taps. Seb stretched and ambled about a bit. He was gangly, all elbows and knees, at that awkward age when you felt like you were always tripping over bits of him. 'Can I watch some telly? *The Bill*'s on.'

'Okay, just for half an hour, then I want you to finish your homework.'

Toby cleared the plates and wiped down the table. He searched through Ginny's bag and found a letter.

'Dear Mr and Mrs Linton,

We have noticed that Virginia's attendance at school has been sporadic over the last three months. We are concerned about the effect this has on her performance, especially as she is due to sit her GCSEs this year. I would ask you to contact the school office to arrange an appointment...'

Toby spread the letter flat and placed it next to the telephone. In Seb's bag he found a note from the Welfare Officer.

'Sebastian's behaviour, particularly his difficulty in being able to concentrate, has been causing concern. We would suggest that tests for the autism and dyslexia spectra may be necessary.'

Toby did the washing up. It was still raining. Outside he could see the dim shapes of the sheets flapping on the clothesline. Perhaps they would be blown off the line, land in the mud and he'd have to wash them again. Ginny came down, wrapped in a dressing gown, hair encased in a towel turban. Seb came in from the living room.

At eight o'clock Seb said, 'I've finished my homework.' He packed the piles of books and ring binders into his bag.

'Okay, go and have a shower.'

'Then can we have supper?'

Hungry again. 'Sure. Now go and wash.'

When Seb had gone Toby set his books on the table. By the time he'd done his work, it would probably be midnight. Ginny settled down to study. He got the two letters and placed them on the table between them.

Ginny looked up.

'Read them.' Toby pointed to the letters. After she'd finished, he said, 'What are we going to do?'

'I'm really sorry, Toby. It's my fault, about Seb. I gave it to him.'

'What did you give him?'

'We smoked some dope. We've done it a few times. I thought it might help him, you know, sleep without, you know…' She made a hissing sound.

Don't get angry, it never helps. Count to three (one, elephant, two, elephant, three, elephant) then take a deep breath. Anything that you say in anger you will probably (always) regret. Toby picked up the letters and threw them at her, his body shuddering as he struggled to keep his voice low. 'Do you want to go into a children's home? Do you think it would be better than this? Tell me, go on…'

'No.' Tears fell from Ginny's eyes. She gripped her arms tightly as if she were a present that was trying to wrap itself.

The flat of his hand landed on the table with a dull thud. 'I'm going to have to ring them.'

'Don't ring them, please. I don't ever want to … not after all this. We made a pledge, didn't we?'

'Yeah, we did.' Toby ran his hands through his hair, pulling it upwards. They had made a pledge that they would keep living in this out-of-the-way house, and they wouldn't tell anyone what had happened so that they could stay together. Most importantly they would never, ever ask their parents for anything again. 'But you've got to help me. Sometimes,' like now, like almost every day, 'I don't feel like I can keep this up.' The stupid thing was he wasn't angry at Ginny or Seb – what fault was it of theirs that they had been born?

'Don't fight against me.' He stopped himself from adding 'or we're doomed.'

'Or we're doomed,' Ginny said, and they smiled.

'No more drugs. And keep eating.'

'Yes, Dad.'

'Don't you start!'

'Write some letters. You're good at forging the signatures. And I'll be better, I promise, no really, I will, it's just that sometimes I feel…'

'I know how you feel…'

'It's just that you never show it.'

Didn't he? He heard Seb calling; what was it – *pyjamas*? Ah, that was it – *no pyjamas.*

Toby pulled himself up (how odd it was to feel so old at seventeen) and climbed the stairs. He opened the hall cupboard. When Dad moved out to live with his new girlfriend, he'd left some of his clothes behind. Not long after, Mum decided to move to France. In the gloom Toby found some of his father's old striped pyjamas. He carried them down the hallway to the bathroom.

Their parents set up direct debits to pay the bills and Toby agreed to look after Ginny and Seb. There was no question of them going to live with Mum or Dad – both parents had made it quite clear that that was not an option. They were no longer wanted, simple as that.

Toby took the pyjamas into the bathroom. Seb was huddled in a towel, enveloped in steam.

'Thanks, bro.'

'Get them on, then come and have your supper.' Toby threw the pyjamas towards him and closed the door.

Katherine and the Lighthouse

Katherine lay in bed next to Jack. Outside the window, light flickered in the darkness and was gone. Could it be the beam of the lighthouse at St Anthony's Head, slipping over her on its dutiful circuit? Did its light reach this far?

Jack read; the pages shuffled as he turned them. Why didn't he turn to her? She glared at the paper as if, beneath the fire of her gaze, she could make it burst into flame. The pages in his hand were more important to him that she was. It came to her that he had no heart; she wanted to press her ear against his chest and listen, convinced that instead of the thump, thump, thump of muscle churning blood she would hear instead the dry rustle of shuffled paper. But if she did that Jack would accuse her of melo-drama.

'Katya,' he'd say, 'really!' And the temperature in the bedroom, in the bed, would sink even lower.

She gave a little tug at the sheets, pulling them closer to

stop the cold seeping in, seeing herself for a moment as a nun that sleeps each night as if preparing herself for death, small white hands crossed over her chest.

A week ago they'd left Zennor, where they'd been staying in a cottage next to Lawrence and Frieda. It had been Lawrence's idea, to live together, to build a writers' community. One night Lawrence had chased Frieda out of doors, a carving knife in his hand, threatening murder. From the window Katherine had seen his naked body in the moonlight as he howled and stamped. Frieda had stopped running and laughed at him, and then they'd both started laughing. Katherine had said to Jack, 'Enough's enough. I can't take any more of this.'

And so they'd moved here, to Mylor, to make a new beginning. Now they had a cottage with a garden running down to a tranquil creek, an orchard where the last of the late blossom still dropped from the trees and, best of all, their own little jetty where Jack tied up a borrowed boat. Yet, at times, she missed the strange golden light at Zennor and Lawrence stalking the cliffs; the way he'd stand facing into the howling wind, arms wide, as if asking to embrace or, possibly, wrestle it. No, Zennor – violent, vivid, lawless – was more Lawrence's style than hers.

And now the memory bothered her. What was worse? The rustle of dry pages beside her, or Lawrence and Frieda screaming, and then the sound of their bedsprings creaking? Katherine turned on her side; beneath her body the bedsprings gave a small, plaintive squeak.

'Katya? Are you asleep?'

Jack's voice startled her. She heard him shuffle the papers, drop them on the floor, then blow out the candle with a gentle 'woh'.

'Tomorrow; we'll talk tomorrow,' Jack yawned.

Katherine held her breath, squeezed her eyes closed. Did he know she wasn't asleep? Did he know if only he'd said 'Katya,' half an hour ago then … stop, don't think of it now – think of tomorrow. She heard a regular lulling sound, Jack's breathing perhaps, or the lapping of water as the tide filled the creek, slapping against the piles of the jetty. Tomorrow Fred was coming. Tomorrow Jack would row their little boat to Falmouth to collect Fred and bring him to her.

The next day was made of blue. No cloud: the sky and the river filled the world; a thick dew evaporated in the sun's heat, and only the long grass beneath the trees in the orchard stayed moist. The birds, open-beaked, threw their heads back and sang, their song falling through the air in sweet drips, like honey.

'Fred spotted the lighthouse as we rowed back from town. Why don't we go and picnic there this afternoon?' Jack joined Katherine on the verandah, hands in pockets, cigarette in mouth, fringe shading his eyes.

'Why not?' Katherine looked down to where Fred lingered amongst the trees in the orchard, touching green leaf after green leaf, and examining them carefully as if they were things he had never seen before. 'How does he seem?'

'He seems … fine.' Jack nodded, as if to underline the word. 'Fine, I'd say.'

Katherine packed a picnic, wrapping a pie and wine and apples and tumblers in a gingham cloth. They paid a fisherman to take them across the wide Carrick Roads to the beach near the lighthouse at St Anthony's Head.

Fred jumped down into the turquoise water, mouth opening in a wide 'O' against the cold. Katherine put her arms around his neck and he waded to the beach. She put her nose against his sunburnt neck, breathing in the bready scent of him. Fred smiled at her before placing her with care on the sand. Jack splashed to the shore, pausing in the shallows to flick them with beads of water.

'We might as well bathe now.' Jack pulled off his shirt.

Fred followed him into the sea. Katherine stayed on the beach, watching them.

Fred's leave was almost over; tomorrow he would begin his journey back to the battlefields of France. Would today be the last day she ever saw him? Would he cease to exist as suddenly as, just over six months earlier, Leslie, her brother, had?

A hay bale, lost somehow from the fields above, was her companion on the beach. The rising tide washed threads from it, and Fred and Jack swam amongst the flaxen strands, slapping them on their heads, larking, pretending to be mermaids. Katherine lay on her stomach. The bright gold of the straw against the turquoise water made her think of the story of Rumpelstiltskin; she was the miller's daughter and the king was Jack, locking her in the tower, making her spin her stories, her gold, out of the heaps and heaps of straw piled at her feet.

She turned her head, peeping under her arm at the men, hearing Fred's laugh carry to her across the water. Why did she feel like they were always hiding the things that they knew from themselves, from each other?

After they'd eaten, Jack dozed on the sand, and Fred said, 'Let's climb to the lighthouse.'

Katherine took his hand, and Fred guided her over the grey rocks. By the side of a narrow path were sparse pines, sculpted like bonsai by the wind. Returning some time later, they found the fishing boat waiting and Jack throwing stones in the water.

Katherine felt a breeze push past her hair. The dining room windows were open; the night air was still warm, loaded with the sweetness of the white stocks that grew by the front door.

'Did you go to the lighthouse?' Jack drained his wine glass.

Katherine looked at Fred. 'Yes.'

'What was it like?'

'Oh.' Katherine pushed some apple peelings to the side of her plate with a small, sharp knife. 'It was tall, smelt damp, as if the waves crashed over it. But they don't.' She studied Jack across the table, his sculpted face, his dark fringe hanging in his eyes; she heard paper rustling and turned, convinced the evening breeze had blown some loose pages off the sideboard.

The more Jack drank the more he talked. Fred, who had said little since they'd returned from their picnic, grew quieter until at last, some time after eleven, he excused himself and went to bed.

Katherine lies in bed next to Jack. Outside the window, light flickers in the darkness and is gone.

Slipping out of bed (her toes curl against the chill wood of the floor), Katherine moves into the hallway. Beneath her feet some boards, as if unwilling to be accomplices, creak. Fred opens his door.

Jack knows what she's like; she's never hidden it from him; to live freely, that's what she wants – freedom at any cost. Unfaithfulness leaves no visible trace; Fred's kisses won't stain her skin like the wet, sooty marks left on the fingers of a fisherman after touching a saithe. Fred stands in the doorway – the moonlight touches him and drains the colour from his body, as if it had already begun its work of turning him from man to ghost. If not now – when?

Katherine moves towards him.

Transport

Ruth and Jason had been in Dublin for three days, roaming the pubs and the late night bars, travelling through the warm, constant mizzle by bus, staying with Cora, Jason's friend from college. It was good of Cora; she'd slept on the living room floor so they could share her single bed. Jet-lagged, Ruth and Jason had squeezed tightly together, listening to each other not sleeping.

Now they were heading south through the outskirts in a hire car paid for (as was the rest of the holiday) by a legacy left to Ruth by her grandmother, along with a last request.

'What's the time now?'

'Seven-ish. It should only take a couple of hours to get to Kerry, isn't that what Cora said?

'Yeah, that's what Cora said.'

As they passed another little low row of houses, Jason sighed.

'If you didn't want to come, you needn't have. You

could have stayed in Dublin.' Ruth looked out the window.

'I *did* want to come.'

He'd rather be out with Cora, supping in one of those cosy Victorian pubs by the Liffey, eating at Eddie Rocket's or Abrakebabra, dancing at that place near the park with the Art Nouveau murals of women, beautiful as flowers, on the walls. But that wasn't what they had come all this way for, was it?

His mobile phone beeped.

'Want me to check it for you?'

'Don't bother.'

Who did he think it would be? Cora?

There were few other cars, some smoking chimneys in the distance, low and incongruous, as if they were glimpsing the funnels of some great ocean liner. As they left the last suburbs behind, all but the road was swallowed in darkness – no lights punctured the blackness, except for the odd glint from a farmhouse window or the reflective moon-eyes of rabbits, foxes, cats.

It was almost ten by the time they reached the town, its centre a cluster of pubs around a main square, their spotlit facades bright with paint, picking out the contours of unlikely mermaids in a town so distant from the sea. Inside the pub they found a blaze of light, an almost tangible wall of conversation split open by the occasional ping and trill of bar-side fruit machines. Hanging on the walls were paintings of horse after famous horse, backed up for good effect by their black and white official photographs, and articles about them cut from the newspaper, and faded rosettes for long-ago victories.

'Shall we have a drink?'

'Oh, yes.' Gran had put a bet on the horses every lunchtime, insisting, when Ruth was staying with her, that she did too. When Ruth had asked her how to choose Gran had said, *Just pick a name you like*.

'Town seems pretty.'

'Horse-centric, though, isn't it? Gives me the creeps.' Ruth stirred the ice in her glass, listening to the high tinkle of cubes jostling against each other and the enclosing glass.

'Those horses look like they're smiling.' Jason nodded to a row of equine portraits made of stained glass.

'They do, don't they? I'm starting to find this a bit sinister.' Why were there so many horses everywhere?

'I don't think they're meant to be sinister. So, do you think we'll find the place?'

Tomorrow they were to find out what they could about Gran's parents and, somehow along the way, choose the place to let her ashes go. 'I hope so. I'm tired tonight. I hope I'm not feeling like this tomorrow.'

A barmaid, wide-hipped and slow-moving, showed them to their room where a double bed awaited them, pushed against the wall.

In the morning brightness, the little town bustled with housewives, men in suits, edgy lines of cars. As they walked down the main street, an enormous truck rattled by, emblazoned with shiny chrome fittings and rows of headlights. Lurid fringes decorated the top edge of the windscreen; statues of saints were Blu-tacked to the carpet-covered dashboard, a silver dazzle of St Christopher medals dangled from the rear-view mirror.

Looking around, Ruth saw that the town sat in a green hollow of rippling hills; it was almost as if, around here, the earth had once been liquid, as swirling as a vortex, and this dip had been the draining point into which everything in the vicinity had been sucked. They found a broken tower, rich with ivy, standing off to one side of the main square; inside it was the genealogy centre.

'Family name?' The woman on the desk had the rounded face, dark hair and light blue eyes Ruth had seen repeated with subtle variations so frequently since she'd arrived.

Ruth gave the name, along with the story of how her great-grandparents had left this place over a century before with their seven sons. The eighth child, Ruth's grandmother, had been born in tropical Queensland. Gran's childhood garden had been full, not of these green grasses and low brown trees, but pink and orange hibiscus flowers, purple-blue jacaranda blossom, yellow-gold mangoes so ripe that they split open when they fell to the ground.

'Great-grandfather's Christian name? Your great-grandmother's? Full names of any of the children that were born here?'

Ruth shook her head, hunching her shoulders against the woman's cold blue stare. Why had she come so ill prepared? Words (heard or imagined?) leapt up in her mind. *Transported, not hung.* Had one of them stolen something? What? A loaf of bread? Which one of them had it been? Shame had lost the names of her seven great-uncles, hidden from her the early histories of her great-grandparents and this town's seven sons.

'I've only the name of the road where they used to live. The number.' Ruth passed a scrap of paper over the counter, heart twisting as she saw the curved and intricate curlicues of Gran's writing on the thin blue paper.

'That road is still there. The houses are much as they were.' The woman unfolded a little map of the town (the free sort, edged with advertisements for butchers and garages and bookmakers) before marking two spots in radioactive-green highlighter. 'And there's the graveyard. By the church. At the end of that same road.'

Outside the light seemed too bright. Ruth squinted against it, feeling her eyes sting as they crossed the road, which streamed with a water-fast blur of silvery cars. It didn't take them long to find the little house standing in the middle of a row, dilapidated as though it had long been abandoned.

'Nine of them lived in there.' Ruth looked the façade up and down; the narrow door, the two small windows above and below.

'It's miniscule. How on earth did they all fit?' Jason, six foot six, would have had to stoop to get in the door.

On the way to Ireland, they had stopped in London to visit Jason's parents, fitting in some sightseeing, which included a visit to the Tower. The Crown Jewels had been a brilliant haze; they'd stood on a conveyer belt and been drawn past them. But the thing that had remained in her mind, more vivid than those extravagant stones, were the steps, accommodating at most only half of her size seven feet, that she'd climbed to enter the tiny rooms where prisoners had lived for years with just a table, a bucket and a bed.

Leaving the house behind they walked on to the churchyard, and then past rows of headstones, seeing no name that could pass as any relation. Lastly, awkwardly, they made their way to a neglected corner where the grass grew long, and a shabby brown structure squatted. The tomb was large, perhaps twenty foot by fifteen, made of some sludge-coloured cement or smooth stone, and the roof was pitched, as if this really were some sort of home, and it mattered that the famously frequent rain would run off it, not pool and cause problems like damp. On the side was just the name 'O'Shea', as simple and final as a story's last full stop.

Jason's phone rang and, as he went to answer it, Ruth looked up at the blank backs of the houses that surrounded the graveyard, at the lace curtains in their windows ruched like prim little mouths: row upon row of child-size terraces without even an inch between the pavement and the front door. There was something mean, something cramped and constricted about it all, as if this place did not care for its people at all but horses, horses.

Coming back across the grass, Jason asked, 'Are you ready? Or do you need longer?'

'This is awful.' Ruth gestured at the brown tomb. 'I can't leave Gran here.'

Jason looked around, as if he were trying to see what she saw. 'What shall we do?'

'We can't take her back to Dublin.'

'We could drive on. Go further west to the coast. Find a cliff or a beach…'

'Do you mind?'

'No, of course I don't mind. Listen, Ruth, it's not … it's not what you think. With Cora. We were friends, that's all.' Jason gave his head a little shake.

Had she got it wrong? She had been tired and worried about this trip, wanting everything to be just right. 'It's good of you, to say you'll go on.'

He gave no sign that he'd heard, just replaced the phone in his pocket. And then he said, 'I wish I could have met her.'

After leaving the town, they drove over a pass, where a mountain loch filled a high, stony basin with water as dark and glossy as obsidian. At the coast, they followed a route along the shore and then out, winding down a road that clung to the contours of a peninsula, until they came to a headland. When they could go no further, Jason pulled the car into a parking place. To one side of them was a group of statues, startlingly white as though the paint were touched up on a daily basis, Christ with arms spread as if to encompass the sea, the two Marys kneeling on either side of him; behind them the slopes of the headland rose, divided into fields by hedgerows of fuchsia, its red, abundant, lantern-like flowers dripping into the haze of green. Before them the ocean twisted and shivered, silver and black.

Had her people ever come to this place? Stood here and

looked out at the ocean? How had they lived in that house, with seven children packed into one room, perhaps one bed? With three, or even four, generations stuffed beneath one tiny roof? Even in death they had been packed tightly together, one on top of the other. And then, somehow, her great-grandparents and those seven sons had broken free, had burst from the steerage cabin of a tall ship ready to disperse, light and glowing as seeds, across a new continent. Her grandmother's house in Brisbane had been raised on stilts; iguanas, their skins like armour, had sunbathed on the corrugated iron roof; the garden had been a green tangle of mango, paw-paw and banana trees. Upstairs, through louvre windows, a stephanotis vine had spilled into the house, each white, night-scented flower as fragrant, fresh and pure as the promise of a new beginning.

'I keep feeling that Gran doesn't belong here.' There was something comforting, hypnotic almost, about the rise and fall of the waves, something breath-like.

'We're lucky, aren't we? There's so much open to us.' From Jason's grandparents, émigrés to England from Hungary in the 1930s, he had inherited warm brown eyes, olive skin. 'But Ruth, it's what she wanted.'

A gust of wind rocked the car, singing high and sweet in the undercarriage.

As they opened their doors, his phone rang. Pulling it from his pocket, Jason glanced at the screen.

The box was in her hands. It had been in her hands the whole way.

'Ruth ... wait.'

She had waited long enough. Down by the water she saw that the waves, open-mouthed as if with hunger, would take what they were given without question.

'Ruth, wait for me, please.' She turned to see Jason pull back his hand, and then his phone sailed over her head, silver-swift as a flying fish, still ringing as it fell into the sea.

A moment later, his fingers resting on her arm, she opened the box and it was done. Down the coast, in the distance, she saw a long beach, a fierce line of white horses dashing onto its shore, and the water beating the sand, and felt the earth beneath her feet hard-trembling as with the pounding of a thousand rushing hooves.

Kangaroos

She'd been dreaming of kangaroos, moving across a wide plain, stirring up dust which sparkled like sunlight falling on a child's freshly washed hair. One of the kangaroos had stopped and looked back at her, waiting until she was close enough to see its eyes, wet and vivid as a deer's, but as soon as she moved it sprang away from her – *away, away, away.*

The ringing of the phone woke her from the dream. Her brother spoke to her and said that she had, after all, been asked for. The news surprised her, the old wounds being canyon-deep. In the taxi, and on the train, and in the long, dark hours on the aeroplane (chasing the night, clamped like a hostage-taker's black glove over half the earth), when she closed her eyes, she could still see the light-filled plain, the mob bounding towards a violet thread of light strung tight between the earth and the great white sky. As before, one kangaroo would turn and wait for her, as if to make sure that she followed, before leaping on.

She had left home as soon as she was eighteen, running twelve thousand miles to the opposite side of the world – *away, away, away.* Under grey skies, so much dimmer than the searchlight-bright sun of home, she crouched under umbrellas, made her nest in minute apartments and kept the past away. At work, she shuffled between grey cells in ghost-littered Victorian institutions. And outside the windows, the city hooted and blared and screamed, as falsely mesmerising as a circus.

When the call came, she realised she'd been waiting for it. During those ten years of crouching, she'd felt the net of the past loosen but never let go. There was no mention of forgive and forget, live and let live, just the summons, as if a long-postponed trial were finally being convened.

Reaching the hospital, muddled by time zones, she held the hand in hers, listening to the breath, which grated in and out as a quiet sea rakes shingle. Somehow, as if they were a thousand miles further north, the hot, dry scent of herbs lingered in the room, amongst the ozone and the bleach.

Her brother, his eyes charcoal-ringed, said, 'It's your turn now.' He got up and walked past her as if she hadn't been away for years but had only popped out to the shops for ten minutes.

The nurse who'd brought her in said 'Not long, now,' and pulled the bedside curtain closed.

Someone shouted, 'Mo! Over here! Bring it over here.'

A tap dripped. A mobile ringtone played the theme tune from *The Pink Panther*. Eyes open, she prayed, *Let me put the past to rest.* The wish for a sign bashed her in the solar plexus, hot as a punch.

Was the pressure on her hand imagined?

Nearby, an alarm sounded.

She squeezed her eyes closed; behind them, the dream had continued, as if she stepped out of a cinema halfway through a movie, only returning in time to catch the final scene. The kangaroos had moved further away, so that they seemed no more than black specks against the horizon, silhouetted like birds against a winter sky. They no longer paused, looking back at her to follow. Then they were gone.

She opened her eyes and, looking around, saw that she was alone on a vast and empty plain.

Oh, Sweet Revenant

In no time at all it was no longer summer but autumn, and the man in the bed was her father, and yet, not. The man in the bed had yellow skin, drawn tight over bone. He had the familiar corrugated brow, the sparse, sandy hair. It was him, after all.

Beyond the window was a morning; the tide filled the harbour. There had been heavy dew in the night, which the sun was now ironing to mist. The outline of the mountain reflected in the water's mirror, and then again in the body of the man in the bed, as if he were becoming landscape.

'Do you want to say goodbye?' her mother asked.

Tessa started to move towards him then stopped. He slept; each breath he took was slow, heavy, wet. She wanted to kiss him, to hug him, to see him look at her again. She didn't want to wake him.

'Do you want to kiss Daddy goodbye?' her mother asked again.

Tessa shook her head. She went out into the hallway

and, picking up her suitcase, walked alone down the road to her Nana's house.

A week passed and then another morning came. Nana sat at the table, her head in her hands, a full bowl of porridge, untouched, in front of her. Aunt Rose stood behind her, holding the back of the wooden chair. Rose turned to Tessa, her face stiff. 'Your father's dead. You'd better go back to bed.'

Tessa climbed back under the covers and pulled the still warm sheets over her head.

She saw him again in his coffin; put a bunch of forget-me-nots into his hand. She touched his face – empty now, eyes shut, closed to her forever.

There were so many people at the funeral that they filled the chapel, spilled out on the road. Tessa walked past them with her mother, who cried, and the people looked at them. She could feel them trying to give her something, but there was nothing they could give. Their eyes, all of their eyes on her; she dropped her head.

A policeman wearing white cotton gloves stood in the roadway. He stopped the traffic to let the funeral procession pass.

After the funeral, her mother went away so Tessa stayed with her Nana. Tessa searched her memory, but she couldn't remember if Nana had been at the funeral, and she couldn't ask. Nana seemed increasingly distracted; sometimes she seemed to have lost the ability to hear; other times she hardly noticed whether or not Tessa was there. Tessa often found her sitting at the table, gazing at the water in the harbour.

'I'm just going out to play in the garden. Nana?'

'Sorry, dear,' Nana spoke at last. 'I was miles away.'

Tessa walked up the road to her old home; it was further up the hill, only a few doors away. Down the concrete steps to the subterranean coal shed, her hand fumbling in a gauze of old cobwebs (she hated the feel of them, like sticky shreds of skin) until she found the spare key that hung, in perpetual darkness, from a rusty nail. Letting herself in by the French doors, she climbed up the staircase to her bedroom and lay in a pool of sunlight on the floor. The house smelt of cold. During these sneaky visits, she had found that she could lie on the faded floral carpet for hours and do nothing more than watch dust spinning downwards as it moved between shadow and light.

After a while she got up and began to rummage. The answer was hidden away – it *must* be. Somewhere in this house full of objects, in a piece of furniture, a forgotten drawer, a seemingly empty cupboard, she would find the answer to all of it, she would find out *why*. The trouble was she did not know what to look for. As Tessa opened the cupboard in the hallway, the hinges creaked; inside was a jar of broken wooden spoons. As she worked her way through the rooms, her pockets filled with a selection of buttons, handkerchiefs and pieces of ribbon.

She found her father's diaries in the otherwise empty belly of an ottoman. As she turned the pages, she became increasingly certain that the answer she was looking for was there, in the thicket of words on the creamy-white pages that smelt of dust and time. Her father's writing was notoriously illegible: it scrawled across the pale plain, a series of awkwardly shaped, hurried letters that almost seemed to move, dancing a peculiar jerky dance. She ran her finger beneath a line, painfully picking out the words.

'Met a fortune teller on the Rue de Rosiers. Told me about my wife.'

And then, further down the page.

'Ridiculous. I've no intention of getting married.'

Her father had travelled in so many different countries. She looked out the window, at the houses nestled between the swaying trees. Each house was separate; each roof, made of corrugated iron, was brightly painted. A quarter of the way up the mountainside the bush started, a fur of greenish black with splashes of yellow gorse, like the skin of some tropical frog. The mountaintop, in silhouette against a sky lumpy with clouds, was supposed to be the body of a Maori warrior. He lay there on his back forever, humps and rocky outcrops forming his head, his knees, his feet, his folded hands. From his stomach a television aerial jagged skywards, an elongated, aerated pyramid.

A strange fear prickled her spine, something instinctive that an animal might feel, snuffling danger on the air. After stuffing the diaries into the ottoman, she made her way into the hallway, hobbling a little because her foot had gone to sleep. On the walls were copies of drawings of people in old-fashioned clothes with unhappy faces, drawn in what looked like blood red chalk. Tessa peered down the empty spine of the staircase at the marble floor below. No one there. But the door she thought she had closed earlier had blown open; dry leaves had drifted in; now the wind scurried them across the black and white marble tiles like wayward mice.

'Where have you been?' Nana's hands were clenched around the spirals of the wrought iron gate. 'I called and called. Were you in the garden?'

Tessa didn't want to lie, so she gave an ambiguous half-nod.

'Your hands are filthy. What were you doing, climbing trees?'

Tessa made her way, in a penitent fashion, to the sink. 'I'm sorry, Nana.' She washed her hands in cold water, digging her nails into the bar of Sunlight soap, its lemony scent released as she scrubbed with the nailbrush until the skin around her fingernails broke and bled.

'Bugger it all; the spuds have gone cold. We'll just have

to put some mayonnaise on them and call it potato salad.'

'That'd be nice for a change.'

'You're a funny wee thing, Tessa Grey.' Nana seemed to see her anew all of a sudden. 'Where on earth did you come from?'

Tessa shrugged, and picked up her knife and fork. 'Would you like me to say grace?'

'Your father used to say grace. We thought he might grow up to be a minister, he was such a solemn little boy.' Nana sniffed, pushing herself away from the table. 'Would you like some sweetcorn chutney, Tessa? Tessa?

Tessa didn't reply. She had gone to a place inside herself, searching for the solemn little boy who had eaten at this same table, who had knelt down beside his bed every night and silently whispered his prayers.

Nana, after a spurt of animation, had gone quiet again. Now, as she dozed in her chair in the front room, the sunlight on her hair bright white, Tessa slipped away and ran up the hill, let herself in with the hidden key and made straight for the ottoman. On the last pages of the second diary, she picked out some new words.

'Oh, sweet revenant. So much to tell, so much ... I didn't know...

The second diary ended with these words, *'Maria tells me she is in love with me.'* Maria was her mother's name. As Tessa flicked through the remaining pages – they were blank – she felt a quickening in her blood; too much time had passed, she had better get back in case. In the last few days Nana seemed slower, as if she were moving through water, not air. Tomorrow she could return again and finish reading the grey-covered books. *Oh, sweet revenant.* Was that a poem? Her father often used to quote poetry.

As Tessa walked down the road, her left ear started burning. According to Nana, it meant that someone was talking about her. An unfamiliar car waited on the road.

Tessa sidled down the pathway, past the wrought iron gate. Through the kitchen window, she saw her mother seated at the table.

'Mummy!'

'Tessa. You gave me a fright!'

She threw herself forward, kissed her mother's cheek. 'Are we going home?' There would be time for everything now. But her mother looked, not at her, but at Nana.

'No, sweetheart. I have decided it is time for me to go and see *my* home and *my* family. It has been many years since I have been able to do this. '

'Can I come with you?'

Maria's gaze drifted over the tablecloth, the teapot. 'I'm afraid it's not possible. You will be better here. School is starting again in a week and in Argentina – you would not be happy.'

'When you will come back?'

'Soon,' Maria grabbed her hands. 'Very soon I will come back and then we will have lots of fun together.'

Behind her, Tessa heard Nana give a low click of her tongue. She backed away from Maria towards Nana, burying her head in Nana's fine wool jumper, pulling hanks of hair forward to cover her face.

'Well,' Maria said.

'Well,' Nana echoed.

'I suppose.'

'That's that, then.'

'I should go. My taxi; the cost will be extravagant!'

There was something like a laugh in her mother's voice; it was as if she were on the verge of breaking into giggles. Tessa peeked out from under her hanging hair. Maria's hands fluttered around her face and then, snapping her compact shut, she brushed a little face powder off her lilac skirt.

'Perhaps you would like to come to the airport?' Maria could barely keep to her seat; she had become so buoyant that she might float away.

'All right then.' Nana pushed Tessa up. 'We might as well.'

For a moment Maria's face became flattened, smooth. But then the smile came back.

'I'll wait for you in the taxi. Don't be long.' Her mother's teeth snapped, and Tessa flinched, as if a crocodile had just slid past her on its way back to its swamp.

'I'll just take my pinny off.' But Nana did not move except to take off her glasses and rub at her eyes. Then she leant her weight on the table, her fingers pushing into the green velveteen tablecloth, denting it.

'That woman! Is that all she was going to say to you? What a thing to do.'

Tessa pushed her hand up the sleeve of her jumper and started to scratch her arms; in her stomach was a sweet and sour sloshing, as if the porridge she had eaten that morning – sprinkled with brown sugar and splashed with the top off the whole milk – was rising up in her throat. In the taxi, it might have come pouring out of her mouth, all over Maria's lilac suit and her black shiny shoes, but it stayed down, forming, instead, a burning band around her heart, so that every breath Tessa took seemed to scald her.

The airport was outside the city, on a long windy plain, with the sea to the south and a long range of hills to the north. At seemingly regular intervals, rifts and gullies spilled down the range to the plain, their edges smooth yet sharply defined: a set of claw-like toes. Tessa stared at them; perhaps they had once been the base of a line of gigantic idols rising up to challenge the sky, like the Moai of Rapa Nui, arms folded against their stone chests, gazing with eyes of white coral and obsidian out to the Southern Ocean, defying invaders that never came to challenge them, defying the wind. And then they had fallen, leaving no trace of their vast bodies, only the platform where once their feet had stood, now grown over with grass and scrub.

Tessa could see the platforms from the windows of the departure lounge. She sat in between Nana and Maria. When the boarding announcement came, Maria bent over and kissed the top of Tessa's head. The smell of L'Air du Temps was Maria's alone, but the face powder and cigarettes could have belonged to any other mother. Her mother's long nails dug into Tessa's shoulder for a moment and then Maria said, 'Goodbye.'

Nana held Tessa's hand as Maria walked through the boarding gate, then out over the runway towards the aeroplane; Tessa felt certain Maria would turn and wave. She didn't.

Side by side on the blue moulded plastic chairs, they waited for the plane to take off. How strange the noise the engines made, both a whine and a roar. The propellers spun faster, faster, becoming a blur; wavering blasts of air, laden with the hot, sweet smell of aviation fuel, streamed from the engines. Faces peeped out from the tiny oval aeroplane windows. Was one of them Maria's? A few hands waved, so Tessa waved back at them. The engine noise got louder, rising almost unbearably until it became a scream, and then the plane moved forward and away.

Tessa stands in the hallway of Nana's house, her suitcase at her feet; she is looking at a faded print of a Redouté rose in a frame varnished sickly yellow.

'It's just until Nana is better,' her Aunt Rose says, 'and then you can come back here. You like it here with Nana, don't you, Tessa?'

Tessa nods. She wishes Rose could move into Nana's house, but Rose says it makes it too difficult to get to work every day. Tessa doesn't like it so much in town, where Rose lives: it is busy, noisy, dirty. In Rose's house, the guest bedroom faces a brick wall; she can't look out of her window at night, when she is supposed to be sleeping, and watch the lights on the sandbanks blink red and green, red and green, marking the way of safety.

After tiptoeing into the kitchen, Tessa stands on a chair so that she can reach into the cupboard above the table. She lifts down the El Dorado biscuit box and opens it. The biscuits have long gone; Nana uses the box to store old photographs. Tessa thinks she hears Rose coming, so she grabs the photograph on the top of the box, a picture of her parents on their wedding day. After shoving the photo down inside the waistband of her skirt, she puts the box away.

'What are you doing, Tessa?'

'Nothing.'

'It's almost time,' Rose says. 'Have you got everything?'

Tessa nods. 'Can I look around the garden before we go?'

'Ten minutes.' Rose's pale blue eyes squint as she checks at her watch. 'I need to empty out the fridge. Don't be long.'

As soon as she is outside, Tessa scoots up the road. The gate, which usually sticks fast, stands open, swinging on new, shiny hinges. A 'For Sale' sign has been pounded into the azalea bed. A noise rises up in her throat; she clamps her lips together to trap it in her mouth. Bounding up the garden steps two at a time, she presses her nose to the window. The front room is empty. It must be a mistake. Why has no one told her? Of course, Nana's words: 'Is that all you're going to say to her?'

She lets herself in with the hidden key and runs through rooms as empty as a stage set. In the hallway, she jolts to a stop in front of a cabinet. No cups, no plates, no small glass animals, waiting for her to grow up enough to be allowed to hold them. She yanks the hall cupboard open. The hinges still creaks, but the jar of broken wooden spoons has gone. She scrabbles across the marble floor and races up the stairs; beneath her hand the wooden banister slides, as warm and smooth as skin. Panting now, stitch pinching her side, she walks through the upstairs rooms; on the carpet, darker patches where the furniture had stood, ghost shapes. How can this be? Who has let this happen?

Empty, every room, empty; her bedroom empty as the inside of a pale shell. Everything gone. Where has it gone? The shelves in the library are bare, but for a grey breath of dust; the ottoman with its belly-full of treasure, her father's diaries, gone.

The wardrobe in her parents' room is built in to the roof space. She opens the door and climbs in before pulling the doors closed behind her. Drawing up her knees up, she places her forehead on them, folding her arms tightly around her legs. Darkness surrounds her, and, in the warm, stale air an almost tangible weight presses down; the last remaining trace of the hours that they have passed there; the last time they will ever be together.

The Day of the Storm

The north-easterly wind had been blowing all morning, warm and plangent, bringing with it ghost smells of warm South Pacific islands, hints of frangipani, wisps of hibiscus. At lunchtime it had turned ugly; because the school lay on an isthmus between harbour and sea, they had been bundled onto buses and sent home early. Tessa watched as the wind picked up the shallow harbour water and threw it across the road as the bus grumbled down the harbour-side road. The tide was unusually high: surface water from vast puddles on the road splashed up, splattering the windows. The sky was paved with thick slabs of cloud; shafts of gold light, squeezing between the cracks, fell like spotlights on the wild, khaki waves and then the clouds split open and great blobs of rain began to pelt down.

'Are you scared?' Tessa asked Cleo.

'Nah.' Cleo sucked the end of a hank of ebony hair. 'Scared of a bit of wind and water? Don't be a derr.'

Cleo barely spoke to her since the last time she had stayed over at the Crofts. Tessa had continued to cling to Cleo, stubborn as a limpet. But what was the point? Picking up her bag, Tessa moved a few rows down to an empty seat. As she sat down she saw Cleo leaning into the aisle, her nasty smile becoming a smirk. Tessa's eyes had gone blurrier than the windows of the bus; she wiped at them with her dirty coat sleeve.

A few weeks ago she had started big school, travelling every day on the bus into town. Her friends had slipped into it all so easily, the khaki and brown uniform, the new routine. Everyone else had forgotten what had happened, but to Tessa it was recent, vivid. Over a year had passed; soon she would be twelve, but she still didn't have words to describe it – it was as if she had woken up one day and the ground had shifted, the mountain fallen, the city been eaten by the sea.

The bus stopped in the middle of a world of rain. Why even try to stay dry? The bus stop jutted out over the harbour and, as she stepped down, wind-driven water lapped over her ankles. Cleo jumped off behind Tessa, splashing and kicking, deliberately soaking her. Ignoring her, Tessa crossed the road, took off her shoes and socks, wrapped her schoolbag in her coat and began to walk up the steep hill to her grandmother's house.

'You look like a drowned rat.' Violet said, opening the door. 'Come in before you catch your death of cold.' She shuffled forward, muttering 'Dear, oh dear' under her breath, as if Tessa had conjured up this day of abysmal weather on purpose, to annoy her. 'You'll have to take those wet things off.'

Violet shooed Tessa into the tile-lined bathroom, Antarctic-white. 'I'll get you some things to change into; put those soggy things in the bath.' And then, a little more kindly, as if some of her crossness had passed, 'Filthy weather. You look like the wreck of the Hesperus. We'd better warm you up, or you'll only be good for boiling down.'

The way Violet talked was cryptic, but comforting, her words like a hand that sometimes stroked, sometimes struck. As Tessa shivered in the frigid air of the bathroom, her skin covered in goose bumps, the door opened and clean underwear and a worn nightdress, a dressing-gown and fur-lined tartan slippers came sliding towards her over the tiled floor.

As soon as Tessa was dressed, her hair wrapped in a towel, she hurried to the kitchen; the scent of tea was acrid, like the piles of wet leaves under the trees in the garden. Violet stood at the counter, spreading butter on thick slices of gingerbread. As Tessa padded up to her, the lights flickered and went out.

'Oh, bugger. The electric's on the blink. I'd better light the stove.'

Tessa helped Violet roll newspaper, make twists of it to feed to the fire. Violet's hands did not bend so much; she worked them like pincers, securing objects between her thumb and the flat of her fingers. Once the stove was going, they sat at the table. Violet stirred her tea, fiddling with her spoon, sighing. Outside the window, the solid shapes of the trees and houses dissolved under the rain.

'It's raining cats and dogs.'

Tessa nodded, biting into a hunk of gingerbread. 'The waves are breaking over the road.'

'No need to worry about us flooding.' Violet picked up a piece of gingerbread then put it down again. 'We'll be all right, up on the hill.'

'They showed us a video at school this morning. About what to do if there is a tsunami.'

Tessa waited for a lecture to begin on the evil effects of television on the young. But not today. Silence, and then Violet got up began to push more paper and cardboard, from her hoard of anything that could be burnt, into the stove. Why wasn't Violet listening to her? Did Violet know what to do if she saw the sea start to draw back, or caught sight of a massive, distant wave? Did Violet know that, if she heard the loud sucking noise that always accompanies a tsunami, it was already too late; too late to run to safety, too late to escape to higher ground? Tessa shuddered and pulled her dressing gown closer against her body.

Above their heads, the clock on the yellow wall chimed five. Outside, no lights; the harbour, the city, even the streetlights, which usually cast orange tap roots down into the water, were lost in liquid darkness.

Nothing.

Nothing.

And then, through the streaming rain, a red light blinked and then a green, red again and green; the pilot lights, set on the harbour's sandbanks, marking the wing-tips of the shipping channel.

'We'd better get the candles out.'

From the kitchen drawer, Violet pulled a box of candles and matches, holding the lit candle horizontally so that wax dripped onto the silver pie tray, before planting the candle upright in the molten pool.

'I'll get the cards then, shall I, Granny?'

'Aye,' Violet said, more with resignation than delight.

They played Fish, then Snap, then Memory. Tessa won every game. Violet didn't seem to be concentrating. Instead she stared out, beyond the circle of candlelight, into the lashing darkness beyond the window.

'Let's play poker.'

Tessa swept the playing cards up, patting them into a rough pyramid with her hands. Violet loved playing poker. Inside a special matchbox, she hoarded the spent matchsticks that they used, instead of money, to place bets. But tonight the atmosphere in the room dropped in steady increments, in time, it seemed, with the ticking of the clock.

Tessa had got used to sensing these changes, these shifts. It was what happened, now. She could feel the unhappiness coming off Violet, as cool and foggy as cloud sliding down a mountain. Last time, Violet had had to stay in hospital for more than six months. You could be sick because you were unhappy: adults were not the rocks she had thought them to be, solid, unchanging, impervious. They could move or break or simply no longer be there. There was no unwritten rule that said life had to keep being good, or keep getting better. Bad things could happen, had happened, could keep happening; that was why Violet had been in hospital, that was why Violet sighed, that was why Violet did not fear the storm; instead, when she raised her eyes at the thrashing weather it was with something like pleasure, her dentures clicking.

'Granny, can we look at the photos?'

'Hmm.'

Tessa had to stand on a chair because the El Dorado biscuit box was kept on the top shelf of the highest cupboard. The biscuits were long gone; inside it were piles of old photographs. Sometimes Violet would clench her hands and push herself away from the table at the very mention of them, but today she stayed seated, staring at the lid of the biscuit box as she had earlier stared at the blackness beyond the window.

Spanish soldiers in dense, lush jungle, piles of treasure mounting at their feet. The candlelight gave the drawing on the box lid another dimension; the bodies of the soldiers seemed to flicker into life, and then she was with them in the jungle while they dug and dug in the steaming earth, their faces leering, the trees crowding at their backs, the air pierced by sudden screeching. A pressure started in her chest, forcing the breath out of her; with a flip of her wrist she turned the box lid over.

Tessa began to lay the black and white photographs on the dark green cloth, as earlier she had dealt out the cards, the action calming her, her breathing and heartbeat slowing.

At the sight of the photos, Violet inclined her head away and sniffed, but her old, knobbly hand stayed on the tablecloth, her fingernails raking its velveteen surface. In the first photograph, two young men and a woman sat on a rock. On the ground before them was a picnic blanket; in the background, a lighthouse on a finger of land reaching into a foaming sea. One of the men looking towards the camera was Tessa's father. The picture was a bit blurred. Tessa wasn't sure if it was her mother with him, or who the other man was. Tessa pointed to it and looked at Violet.

'Nugget Point. Your father was having an outing with some friends. Can't remember why, now.'

The next photo was of a slim, vaguely pretty girl in a satin ball gown, with a large orchid corsage pinned to her shoulder strap. Tessa's finger moved to it.

'That was your aunt going out to the Phillip Perkins Christmas dinner.'

The next photograph was one of a series; it was an obsession of hers to find them all and line them up. It showed a man, Tessa's father, sitting on a camel. In the background squatted the unmistakeable receding shapes of the pyramids of Giza, sticking out of the desert like pointed teeth. On the right of the camel a palm tree, laden with dates, and the small shape of the camel driver swaddled in white robes. Another photograph showed a line of camels in the distance, Tessa's father still possibly riding on one of them, it was impossible to tell, and looming over them, like a lion over a trail of ants, the crouched feline body and inscrutable visage of the Sphinx.

When the stove was hot, Violet heated them vegetable soup. Bits of barley got stuck between Tessa's teeth. The soup glowed inside her stomach like a warm secret, as comforting as the hot tea had been earlier. The storm showed no sign of abating: it howled in the darkness, clawing at the house; its ferocity dismayed her; she had never known its like for sheer intensity. Perhaps, this time, it would not end, but just go on and on.

'You can come in with me tonight.' It was as if Violet could sense her fear; it felt like the kindest thing anyone had ever said to her.

Violet put her false teeth in a glass of water by the bed. She swallowed a little white pill then, curling up, she pulled Tessa to her and fell straight to sleep, her breath a warm growl on the back of Tessa's head. But Tessa could not sleep. She lay in the dark, hearing the nocturnal clicking of the house and the lash and whistle of the storm: its beating and abating had a rhythm of its own, a peculiar music, as it broke over the house, stamped on the trees, flattened the bushes in the garden.

At some point Tessa fell into a waking, walking kind of sleep. She dreamt that she was standing on the terrace in front of the house, looking down on the harbour. For a moment she raised her eyes to the mountain with its profile of a fallen warrior, a great chief lying on his back, arms folded across his chest. Then she noticed the water had begun to rise; soon it would flood the terrace, now it lapped warmly around her ankles. Looking down she could see flowers floating in it, just below the surface. She reached down to scoop the flowers up, but as she touched the water's surface it began to recede. It disappeared quickly, dropping within minutes to the level of the road and then further, like a bath draining. Sandbanks appeared and the shores of the harbour as they were at low tide, with their pink volcanic lava flows, muddy puddles full of mermaids' necklaces and cats' eyes, and still the water went out, further than Tessa had ever seen it go.

Shapes began to appear, indistinguishable at first, covered in mud, but revealed as the light hit them: an old bicycle; the remains of a tall ship, its crippled masts snapped and tangled into a lopsided wigwam; a car, standing on its nose, creaking as the wind hit it and began to push it over; tea chests; containers; a small fishing boat with a blue hull and the name 'Evangeline', a ragged hole ripped in its side.

Now Tessa was walking on the floor of the harbour amongst oars, planks of barnacle-covered wood, lobster pots, wreckage and scrimmage and no-name things, pyramids of jumbled stones, and there a wooden box, a coffin, there it was, the thing that up until then she did not know she was looking for – there, there. She just needed to reach it, to step across the gap, but there was a large puddle in front of her, stopping her. As she watched, the coffin started to move away from her, pulled by the shallow, remaining tide.

Where were the roses? It should have been covered in roses. Where were the flowers she had seen? She heard a noise, ferocious as the sound of a train approaching, and turned to look over her shoulder. It wasn't a train but a wall of water: high, wide, fast. There was no time, no time for anything more. She turned to look once more at the coffin, being pulled away from her now down the pathway to the sea, and then closed her eyes and waited for the water to hit her, a whimpering sound in her throat trying and failing to break free.

Bright, Fine Gold

'm off for a walk,' I call to Anna, as I pass down the hallway.

In my peripheral vision, I see a flash of my face reflected in the mirror that hangs above the fireplace. Anna raises her head from her books, tilts her pencil away from the paper. The clock on the mantelpiece ticks once, twice and the wind spins down the chimney, breathing on the coals, making them glow. If words rise her in throat, she traps them quickly behind her teeth. And then the high-ceilinged room is behind me; the gilt-framed mirror above the fireplace reflects nothing but a patch of white wall, the top angle of the doorframe. In an essay, one of my pupils once wrote *guilt* instead of *gilt* – a guilt-framed mirror. Yes, I thought, it can be.

My gloves, hat, coat already on, I open the front door. I try not to think of Anna rising from her desk, moving to the bay window, gazing out into the snow-light. Beneath my feet, a layer of new sleet crunches as I skid down the path.

I cross the main road quietly; all around me, the little town of Tuapeka sleeps. One hundred and fifty years ago, gold was found in the river here, 'Shining like the stars in Orion' the miner said, 'on a dark, frosty night'.

I walk into the gully where the miners once camped, thousands and thousands of them. When people drive through this town, they see the old shops with their Wild West-style wooden verandas set, seemingly without reason, amongst green hills. The whole town turns its back on the river, as if there were something shameful about it.

Today the river's the pale greyish-green of a wax-eye's back. The stones are furred with frost. Where does the light come from, on a day like this, when the sun barely manages to haul itself over the horizon?

As I walk the shore, snapping dry grass stems and feeding them to the water, I think of Anna waiting by the window, arms folded tight against her stomach.

Last night, after we'd eaten lamb casserole and drunk enough red wine to whet the slicing edge of our tongues, Anna said, 'We can talk about it, you know. We can do something, together, to remember her. This day comes around every year...'

'Please.' I raised my hand. 'Please, no more.'

After I heard Anna's feet on the stairs, I got the flashlight and went into the pantry. Tilting my head underneath one of the shelves, I ran the beam of light over the words, *Siobhan was here. Siobhan was here.*

She'd written it twice, as if it bore repeating, as if, even then, when she was only thirteen, she'd known already that her grip on the world was tenuous.

I sat for a long time, reading the words. And then I turned the flashlight off and sat in the dark.

I've never seen the river freeze, even in the coldest winter. Siobhan and I used to sing a song about the Gold Rush, when we spent our time here. We had learnt it at school, along with every other child in the province of Otago.

Bright, fine gold
Bright, fine gold
Whangapeka, Tuapeka
Bright, fine gold.

Still young enough to believe in the kind of miraculous gain made possible solely by youthful ingenuity, we spent one summer gold-panning. And we did find gold, but only tiny flakes of it. Siobhan had read somewhere that it could be eaten; she made me pick each flake out of the sludge and swallow it so that nothing would be lost.

Doesn't it just come out? I must have already been in love with her or I would have said something like 'crap it out'; in those days, swear words had the same hard buzz as exploding candy on my tongue.

As we stood in the river, day after day, the sun hot on our backs, up to our knees in water, sluicing the gravel, Siobhan sang, her voice as plangent as that of an old miner who sleeps each night on frozen ground;

I'm weary of Otago
I'm weary of the snow
Let my man strike it rich
And then we'll go.

Something glitters under the water, so I wade in, once more, over the old stones until I'm up to my knees. *Siobhan was here.* I plunge my hand, still gloved, through the surface and make a grab at it, but whatever it was that glimmered there has gone.

Above me, the clouds have turned yellow-grey. As the first snowflakes start to drop, I stick out my tongue to taste them. The river does not miss her, nor does the snow. Perhaps, if I stand here long enough, I can freeze her out of me.

Now the snow falls thickly, covering the grey stones; it falls on my shoulders, and my forearms; it coats my hat in a crown of ice.

We shared a flat, Siobhan and I, in our last year of university. Always one to follow her heart, she studied Geology. I wanted to do something special for her, as a graduation present. She had read about the scenic flights to Antarctica in the paper, and she wanted to go there. *Imagine, Patrick, a place like that, frozen in time. There are active volcanoes there, did you know?*

Yes, I knew. I'd gone through a stage of being fascinated by vulcanology, somewhere after my early obsession with carnivorous dinosaurs ended and my all-consuming bedazzlement by Siobhan began.

I only had enough money for one ticket, so I gave it to Siobhan.

Something makes me move – my skin is so cold it's burning, and I shiver and move away from the river. I hurry along trying to stamp some warmth back into my feet. I can see lights, yellow as butter, in the windows of the houses. Crossing the road, I stumble up to the door of the house next to mine and knock.

After a moment, Siobhan's father answers. 'Patrick. Look, I've told you…'

'Please,' I say, 'please?' Their house smells, as always, of warm Ribena.

'Margaret?' He half-turns and shouts behind him down the hallway, 'Patrick's here. Look at the state of you, what have you been … all right, come in, but only for a moment.'

Siobhan's mother comes and stands next to her husband. 'Patrick, we told you last time … what happened? You're soaked.'

'I saw something in the river and…'

'Patrick – this has got to stop. It's been thirteen years. You need to make your peace with it.'

'Can I go in … please?'

'No, Patrick, we told you. Her things are gone. You have to let go.'

58

They used to let me sit in her room.

'I didn't mean to; I know I promised … it's just that today, today…'

'Go home to Anna. And Patrick, get those wet things off quickly or you'll catch your death of cold.'

As he closes the door, her father whispers, 'It's hard enough. Please, leave us alone.'

There's a pause between the last two words, as if he almost said, '…leave us *all* alone.'

Outside, I put my head down; snow sweeps across the valley, driven hard and fast by the southerly wind. It was nothing more or less than an accident. The flight plan was changed in error, and the plane was allowed to fly low, so the passengers would have better views. Visibility was so poor the plane flew straight into the side of Mt Erebus.

I open the door, shrug my wet layers off.

'Anna? Anna?'

No answer. She's gone. *I'm weary of Otago, I'm weary of the snow.* She's taken the car. Are there trains anymore? There used to be trains, when Siobhan and I … *Anna,* I'll say when I see her again, I'll go down on my knees, *please forgive me. It's just that … it's just…*

There must have been miners amongst the thousands, mustn't there, who toiled for years but found nothing – was this what it was like for them? What kept them going? How many winters did it take for them to lose hope, to throw down their picks and pans, abandon their tents and head for home?

As I feed the fire and pour some whisky, the room fills with the colours of life – leaping flames as orange and twisting as barley sugar, the liquid glinting amber against the light-slicing cut-crystal, my cranberry-red defrosting feet.

I go to Anna's desk and rummage for her sister's telephone number. When she's doing her research, Anna peppers her books and journals with Day-Glo pink, orange and green Post-it notes; some end up as jungle-bright and frilly as carnival costumes. Anna is a garden designer – she's planning to plant an area behind the house; somewhere we will be able to sit in the summer and glimpse the river as it twists amongst the willows. I see notes, in her careful hand, on a white sheet of foolscap: *Naturally occurring gold is found in honey-bee pollen – plants with high levels of gold include* Brassica juncea *(Indian mustard), a hyper-accumulator, which stores up to 100 times more gold than associated plants.*

I flip over a few loose sheets of paper photocopied from some scientific journal and see, highlighted in fluorescent yellow marker pen; *07 September 1991. Mount Erebus ... in Antarctica is spewing out tiny crystals of gold ... although other volcanoes are known to emit gold, Mount Erebus is the only one to emit it in metallic form...(1)*

On the phone, I tell Anna that she's right. That I'm sorry. That it's time. That I want to move away from here. That we will plant the garden she's designed elsewhere. I tell her I no longer want to be the person I saw reflected in the mirror, in the water, in Siobhan's parents' eyes. I tell her that I don't want this to keep happening every year, for this day to be the end of the world for me as well. I ask if I can come and see her in town tomorrow, take her out for dinner because there is something very important I want to ask her.

After ringing Anna, I fall asleep in front of the fire. I dream of Siobhan, standing in the river; in her hands she holds a nugget of softest, purest yellow. Raising it to her mouth she swallows it, and then she smiles at me, her widest smile. And then I see her standing on the snows, while all around her falls a fine yet dazzling rain.

One of the Best

A little while ago, I acquired (or I probably should say re-acquired, because they were, after all, mine to begin with) a folder containing my old school reports. Although they were more than twenty years old, the reports themselves, apart from a coating of what appeared to be dry, flaky dirt, were still legible. What surprised me most, reading back through them, was how clear some of those years – some days, even – still seemed to me now, compared to others, which were total blanks. But one of the two years I spent at Taiaroa Intermediate, though arguably the most difficult in my life, was also one of the best.

Taiaroa was a kind of waystation for school children aged eleven and twelve, a stepping stone between primary and high school, a two-year respite before the dual onslaughts of hormones and exams. In the first year my teacher was Mr Moon and, though I loved him, I had also found him mercurial. A newly minted father, convinced that his firstborn was destined to be the new Messiah, he seemed to find us, his class, underwhelming, a speckled, uninspiring lot. And for me, the personal changes of that year in particular were many; at the centre of them was a new and devastating absence.

It was then, also, that my mother began to forget to pick me up from places. I did not have to be collected from school because a bus took children who lived in outlying villages home, but if I had to stay late for netball or athletics or drama or choir then I was frequently the only child left at the school gates and, more often than not, a call had to be made to remind my mother to come and get me. Despite the repeated phone-calls, and perhaps at one time an interview with the Welfare Officer, this pattern went on into my second year when Mr Hermitage became my teacher.

When our class went away for a week on school camp and were scheduled to return on a Sunday, perhaps worried that he would have to wait for hours for my mother to show up on a day when the administration office would be closed, Mr Hermitage said that he would drop me home.

After camp, all the other children were collected by their parents except for me and Lincoln. Lincoln was slight and freckly. We had 'gone out' together for a short time, probably, as was usual at that age, a matter of days or, at most, a week. I was taller than him, as I was taller than nearly all the boys in my class, though, having had a series of illnesses, I was also on the thin side. Mr Hermitage was covered by a pelt of thick dark hair that only seemed to break to let the features of his face peek out. If he hadn't diligently shaved, my imagination warned that he may be mistaken for an escapee from the *Planet of the Apes*. Oddly, there was a bald patch on the inside of each shin where, he said, the socks he'd worn each day as a schoolboy had permanently rubbed the hair on that part of his leg away.

Lincoln sat in the front seat; I was in the back. Mr Hermitage's car was sporty, red, sitting low to the ground.

Mr Hermitage said, 'Remind me where you live again, Lincoln?'

'Waverly,' said Lincoln.

'I'll drop you off first then,' Mr Hermitage said.

My heart clenched at this. If Mr Hermitage dropped Lincoln off first then I would be left alone in the car with him. This was awkward because I might be expected to talk to him, and I hated talking to adults. Also for logistical reasons – I was in the back of a two-door car – when Lincoln got out should I get in the front seat or remain in the back like an imbecile or toddler? But for some reason, Mr Hermitage did not turn off the harbour road to Waverly. And now my dilemma changed; when we arrived at my house would Mr Hermitage, or even, God forbid, Lincoln, want to come inside?

The best outcome would be that they would merely drop me at the top of the drive and, without more than a goodbye, speed away. If my mother wasn't home I would wait in the garden, as I often did after school when I was locked out of the house. If it rained, I would wait in the old wash house; no longer used for washing, it was warm and dry with three long shelves under the window where my father used to store the dahlia tubers he dug up from the garden each winter, and shallow trays filled with white Borax powder to preserve velvet-petalled, deep purple pansies forever.

On the top shelf I ran a kind of nursing home for specimens of light-deprived, over-watered plants from my mother's shop. There I'd dry out cyclamen corms and coax maidenhair ferns back to life, catering to each in terms of its requirements of light, shade, water, clustering them together so their leaves overlapped, a little potted garden, intimate and tactile as a close-knit family. It was also a favourite refuge of my cat; in fact his official bed was out there. If I was tired I could lie down with him, under the lowest shelf. It was so cosy that I admit I sometimes fell asleep there too.

When we arrived at my house, Mr Hermitage turned into the drive and, pulling into the carport, parked his car next to my mother's acid green Starlet. Lincoln popped the seat forward to let me out; Mr Hermitage pulled my bags from the boot. I flung the door open and yelled, 'Mum!'

As I turned I thumped into Mr Hermitage who already stood on the porch, bags in hand.

'Thank you for bringing Ellie home.'

'What a lovely house.' Mr Hermitage angled his body so he could peer behind her down the wood-panelled hall-way.

'Would you like to come in for a cup of tea?'

'A cup of tea is exactly what I would like.' Mr Hermitage followed my mother inside, turning to shout, as if calling a dog to heel, 'Lincoln, here.'

Lincoln sped past me, not catching my eye. After I had dragged my bags down the hall to the utility room, I dashed out to the wash house. My mother had forgotten to water the plants. Some of their leaves were dropping, some burnt by the sun. After giving them a lightning splash of water, I ran back inside.

I found my mother, Mr Hermitage and Lincoln in the front room, light flooding through the picture window, the harbour beyond it calm and green. Lincoln sat on the gold and blue brocade sofa, his feet not quite touching the ground, his knobbly knees covered in dirt though less wretchedly filthy than the trainers dangling from his too big feet, his mouth hanging open as he glanced from the gleaming black wood of the baby grand piano to the soft glow of the silver on the sideboard, from the cabinet filled with rose-coloured Venetian glass to the Chinese screen embroidered with grey and brown silk sparrows flitting through dangling clusters of wisteria. A blush tore across my face; starting at my nose it flamed across my cheeks before setting my ears on fire. My mother and Mr Hermitage were deep in conversation, as apparently unaware of my presence as they were of Lincoln's. As I was about to sneak out of the room, my mother said, 'Mr Hermitage will have a cup of tea.'

Mr Hermitage said, 'Lincoln will have something cold. Juice, perhaps.'

He'd be lucky, I thought, skulking back to the kitchen, and there's never any tea.

I liked the kitchen; it was cool and dark, with encaustic tiles on the floor and marble worktops. I opened the fridge, relieved to find half a pint of milk in it, then opened the freezer and pulled out the jar of ground coffee, squat as a funerary urn, which sat in the middle of the otherwise empty space as if in a white palace of frost. After wrestling two espressos from the elaborate coffee machine, I poured the milk into a glass, trying to ignore the fact that it was a watery yellow colour and smelt worse than a dead lamb. I slammed through the cupboards, knowing I would not find any biscuits in them. After handing out the drinks, I sat as far away from the rest of them as possible, looking out of the side window into the garden, focusing my mind on the possible whereabouts of my cat.

After some time they left.

One evening, the following weekend, the phone rang. As I picked it up I could hear my mother pad up behind me, humming gently.

'Ellie?' The voice was familiar.

'Hello, Mr Hermitage.'

'Is your mother there?'

'Just a minute.' After I passed the phone to her, I went out to the wash house, pulled some yellowing leaves off the plants and looked for signs of new growth, or best of all, the curled beginning of a flower that always made my heart swell. But despite the fine weather, there weren't any, as if the plants were still recovering, or perhaps in a sulk after the week of neglect.

As the term went on Mr Hermitage's phone calls to my mother continued, and my mother's absences grew more frequent. Sometimes I only realised she'd been out at all when I woke at the sound of her car returning down the gravel of the driveway and, pulling back the curtains, saw the red flash of brake lights or heard the sound of the Starlet's engine dying.

One day at school, as I was about to go out to lunch, Mr Hermitage asked me to stay back in the classroom, a request that made my heart slam against my ribs. My friends were outside on the lawn throwing a cranberry red cricket ball around; I longed to be out there with them, to lose myself among them.

'Sit down, Ellie.' Mr Hermitage motioned to the seat next to his desk. He was smiling at me but it wasn't a happy smile. Had I done something wrong? I looked down at his legs, my eyes fixing on those two patches on the inside of his shin where the skin was shiny white.

'How are you, Ellie?'

My throat was so dry it felt as though it was lined with bristles. 'Uhnu. I'm fine.'

'The reason I kept you back was that I was very impressed with your project. Very impressed.'

Each month we were given an assignment; usually it involved written and creative work alongside science and other subjects – write a story, make a plan, create a world, use timetables, graphs, charts, that sort of thing. This month we'd had to write about someone stranded on a desert island. I had written a story about a boy called Dougal, who, finding himself alone, perhaps the survivor of a shipwreck of or some other catastrophe too traumatic to recall, collects seeds washed up from distant places and plants, in the shade of the island's trees, a garden, living on coconuts in the meantime.

A bird, similarly blown off course on its way to some other, better place, becomes his companion after he saves its life by sharing his seeds with it, and in this bird, Dougal finds the companionship without which we all shrivel up and die. Dougal and the bird have a series of adventures, discovering that they are able to help each other so satisfactorily that, when rescue comes, Dougal does not want to leave his island, or his bird, behind; he has his garden and the true and faithful friend he needs. Although he re-establishes links with the outside world, he chooses to spend the foreseeable future in happy isolation from the rest of humankind.

'This is a very good story,' Mr Hermitage said. 'You've really grasped Dougal's feelings and how to show his character through his actions.'

'Uh nugh.'

'It's as if you can imagine exactly what it would be like to be trapped on a desert island but still make the best of it.'

'Hnuh.'

'This would make a great children's story. You could try and get it published. Perhaps you'll be a writer when you grow up.'

'Thank you.' Proper words finally though I felt as if I'd swallowed a beach-full of sand.

'I've given you an A+. I've never given any student an A+ before. I expect you want to go and play.'

Mr Hermitage gave a long and surprisingly loud sigh, as he glanced out at the green grass of the playing field, the white shirts of the children racing past the window, the dull red whirr of the ball. Standing, I shuffled backwards, trying not to trip over the rows of desks, thinking I must drink some water so my kidney trouble did not come back when Mr Hermitage said, 'Ellie, wait a moment. Tell me something. Does your mother leave you at home alone a lot? Is it too much?'

Bursts of some cold fire raced through me. Now was the time. As I poured out my answer the cricket ball smashed through the classroom window, shattering it to pieces.

After that, something went wrong. My mother would no longer make small mentions of Mr Hermitage. He would not ring and ask to speak to her, as he had done, in the early evenings; instead he'd sometimes call as late as ten or eleven at night.

He'd say, 'Is she there?'

Fuzzy-headed, I'd check the carport and then say, 'Yes', or 'No.'

On the rare occasions she was in, he'd say, stiffly, 'Please ask your mother to come to the phone.'

I'd go and find her but she'd shake her head, press her lips together and grimace at me.

'Sorry.'

'It's okay, Ellie,' Mr Hermitage would say. 'I'll see you tomorrow.'

Once he came to the house but she wouldn't see him then either, and told me not to let him in.

There were perhaps three more projects I handed in to Mr Hermitage, but I never got an A+ again. The comments were usually good and encouraging although one time, not long after my mother began to refuse to take his phone calls, I got a B-, the closest I'd come to getting a C. Once again Mr Hermitage called me aside to discuss my work. This time the project was about an underwater world where everyone lived under a dome at the bottom of the sea.

After pointing out all the faults he'd found with the world I'd created (the most urgent being, 'How are they supposed to *breathe* down there, Ellie?') Mr Hermitage said, 'It's good for you to know that you can't get top marks for everything you do. It's one of the most important lessons you can learn. It will spur you on to do even better next time.'

Perhaps it was a spur because for quite a while I rarely got lower than an A in anything. I even won a scholarship to attend a fee-paying high school. The only time I voluntarily spoke to him was to tell him, in the last week of term, this news, the words sliding from my throat so smoothly it was as if they had been rubbed with oil.

'My first scholarship pupil,' Mr Hermitage said, 'and it's you, Ellie. Well done. You know, don't you, that you've got a very bright future in front of you.'

After high school, and a rickety ride through university, I went away, and began to live a precarious kind of half-life in the big city at the other end of the country. When I could afford it, I returned to my hometown. On one such visit, about fifteen years after I had been his pupil, I saw Mr Hermitage in Pak'n'Save, standing in front of a red and gold wall of canned chopped tomatoes. He was instantly recognisable: the glasses, the rampant black hair, the fluorescent running shorts, even those bald patches on the inside of his shins. For a moment I wanted to rush over and say hello to him, but what would I say if he asked me what I done with my life? Could I tell him about the bed-sit I lived in between a pub and a kebab shop? Would he think I was making a joke if I told him about the large orange slugs that crawled, without fear, across the carpet in the middle of the night? That despite my degree all the jobs I'd had had been menial? That the children's story I'd sent out to every publishing house in the country had been returned, only one of them bothering to put a slip in saying that they'd enjoyed it at all? It was impossible.

Not long after that visit my mother finally cut me out of her life as effectively, and with as little explanation, as she had Mr Hermitage. *Tell her I'm not here,* her voice whispered in the background, loud enough for me to hear when a man I didn't know answered her telephone.

But recently I was drawn back to my hometown once more, perhaps for the stupid, sentimental reason that I have not, even after more than twenty years, been able to shake off the insistent feeling I am under some sort of obligation to return to the place where I had my beginnings, and to stand, for a short while, in a small cemetery between the rising hills and the harbour water.

After I had been to the cemetery, I stood on the road outside my mother's house. I walked up the road and looked in the carport. Empty. I walked into the garden of my childhood; it was as neglected as ever, even more overgrown. In the wash house, on the top shelf, a row of plants, brown and dry, crumbling to dust. On my hands and knees I lifted a loose board covered by the old moth-eaten blankets of a long-dead but once beloved cat; there, in that cavity, were my school reports. I had arranged them neatly in blue folders filled with plastic sleeves but still, over the years, dust had settled on them, coalescing into dirt. And so I read again the report that Mr Hermitage had written at the end of the year when he had been my teacher.

Ellie has a wealth of academic potential. A gifted and talented writer, I will always remember her as one of the best! Gabriel Hermitage.

There was a tearing feeling on the inside of my throat. He'd felt sorry for me, hadn't he? Knowing or guessing what my life was like, he had tried to bolster me. But that year when he had been my teacher had been, compared to what came later, a golden time. And what luck for him that he had not gotten permanently tangled up with my mother. His words, even if they had not been true, had been a comfort, along with my warm, foul-breathed fur-ball of a cat and that cluster of sickly plants, as well as in the comfortless times that I did not then understand lay ahead of me.

One of the best, I thought.

Yes.

Painting Katherine

When I come into her room she's standing by the window shivering; she's thin, too thin. 'Kate? Katie? How are you?'

She turns to me, arms open. 'Annie.'

From my bag I pull oranges and caramels, piling them up until they form two pyramids on either side of a vase bursting with yellow irises. 'I bought you some treats.'

Katie claps, excited as a child but then she coughs and coughs. Patting her back, I help her to a chair. When she's got her breath back, she says, 'Coffee, Annie? They'll bring it if I ring.'

'Let's just talk. Relax a bit.'

She shakes a cigarette from the packet lying on the table then offers one to me. 'Jack sent me some gaspers. Fancy a Spanish grenade? They're supposed to be good for me.'

From the open window comes the reek of sea, a pungent, pissy smell; is that what makes Katie curl her nose? Smoke trickles from her mouth, as if she were too weak or too lazy to blow it away.

'I thought I might paint your portrait while you're here; what do you say to that?'

'Paint me? Like this? How can you bear to, Annie?'

'I don't see why not.'

'Don't you? That's funny. That's the funniest thing I've heard for I don't know how long.' She grinds the cigarette out in a green glass ashtray, already choked with butts, making a gesture with her hand as if she were brushing some feathers away from her face. And then she says, 'You might paint what's left of me, I suppose.'

She always talks that way, as if she doesn't care a bit.

The diagnosis is pleurisy. Outside, a gorgeous spring's dispensing its own medicine, a string of warm blue days. Katie's told to rest and eat and do *nothing* else. I fill her room with bluebells. She says they smell like honey. An elderly maid, her skin as crumpled and brown as a walnut shell, brings Katie gooseberry jam on thin slices of buttered bread cut into little triangles. *Food to lure fairies from their lairs*, Katie calls it.

When Jack says he's too busy to visit her, Katie erupts. She can be *vile*; she takes most of it out on Jack (he *is* her husband, after all) and some on blameless me and then she cries and asks me to forgive her just like some wayward child. But sick people *are* often difficult, don't you find? So I bring more bluebells and pray for patience and remember how she was when I first met her in Paris. The thing is she can't bear to be apart from Jack, but he's no nurse. So it's tug-of-war letters as usual, though her claws are blunted by her coughing, her struggle to put on and keep on even a few ounces, let alone a pound.

Next time I visit, she says, 'Clotted cream for tea.'

Someone has sent her a boatload of marigolds.

A few weeks later, when Katie's finally out of bed, she

asks, 'What shall I wear in your painting, Annie?'

'Whatever you like.' I'm laying my paints out, feeling the familiar ritual soothe me. I love the moment *before,* a blank canvas waiting on the easel beside me.

Katie leans on the armoire, flicking through dresses. 'Shall I play the dutiful wife? Or the vamp?'

The brick red dress she holds makes her look pale but it's cheerful at least. 'Vamp,' I say, 'definitely the vamp.'

'Do you think there's ever been a vamp in Looe before?'

'I really couldn't say.'

Emerging, changed, from behind the screen, she takes her place. I've surrounded her chair with flowers, bowls of red rhododendron, vases of musk-pink campion. My brush strokes the canvas with a sweet hush, as soothing as a lullaby. Through the open window, in the silver-blue dazzle, gulls cry as if they understand exactly how much she has to lose.

As I work, Katie studies me. 'I'm getting *your* portrait, Annie. I've already got your bronze skin, now I've got those periwinkle eyes. Don't think I haven't got you.' She smiles nastily, a cat with a mouse in its sights.

The painting is done. Not long after, impatient as ever, she's flashed back to Jack in London, to feed on him and make him fail to give her what she needs.

And her portrait?

If I'm honest, I find that it still pleases me. Time's wicked ways stand still there, for an instant at least, as Katie made them do in her stories. And now she's gone, I like to remember her as she was that blazing blue, late Cornish spring, still frail but each day growing stronger, trembling on the edge of another summer.

A Piece of Cake

That day, drizzle fell from a low sky, but there was no wind to hurry the rain away from town and south to the sea or west to fall quietly upon the mountains. Head down, Sophie counted puddles. As they passed their neighbour's house, Sophie's mother, seeing the bottle of milk still perched on the doormat, paused and said, 'I think you'd better go and see Mrs P. today.'

'Do I have to?' Sophie tugged her mother's hand. All day at school she had been waiting for the moment when she would return home, shut the door to her room and play, just play, and not have to think about anything real.

'She always has nice cakes. You like cake. Go on, then.' Her mother, lifting the brown leather school satchel from Sophie's shoulder, gave her a little push.

'But…' Sophie began before a look from her mother silenced her.

Mrs P. was from Poland. Her real name was Przybyszewski, a name that looked like a thorny hedge and was impossible for most people to remember, let alone pronounce. Mrs P. slicked her hair into a low bun at the nape of her neck; when you got close to her, it gave a faint, oily, medicinal smell as if she'd smeared something like Vicks Vaporub on it.

From the outside, Mrs P.'s house looked just like theirs: a brick bungalow, a porch with an opening curved like a keyhole. Climbing the three low steps, Sophie saw what she always saw – Mrs P.'s pile of neatly stacked firewood – and beside it, a pair of men's gumboots standing on age-yellowed newspaper. The boots were filled with layer upon layer of grey spider webs, the hollow bodies of insects dotted through them. After picking up the silver-topped bottle, Sophie knocked on the door.

'Mrs P.?'

No answer. She knocked again.

'Mrs P.?'

Sophie jumped off the porch and started walking down the path, pulling up her hood against the rain, when she heard the sound of the front door rasping against the mat.

'Sophie.' Mrs P. had a hissy kind of voice, like the sound a snake might make if it tried to sing. 'I must have over-slept. Come in, dear.'

The funny thing was, Sophie thought, stepping over the threshold and brushing her feet with care on the bristly orange mat, Mrs P. looked awfully tired. Charcoal shadows ringed her eyes – *Owl eyes,* her mother called them, the unmistakeable result of lack of sleep or symptom of imminent illness. Mrs P. took the milk from Sophie with hands that shook, but then, with a gesture as familiar as a smile, she pulled herself up straight, seeming to reset the angle of her head so that it was square upon her shoulders.

'What time is it?'

'Three-thirty,' Sophie guessed.

'Then we will have afternoon tea.'

After hanging her coat on the hook by the door, Sophie

followed Mrs P. down the hallway to the kitchen. The carpet had a damp smell that reminded Sophie of those dirty yellow toadstools that grew, clumped together, in the mossy margins of the lawn. As she put on the kettle, Mrs P. said, 'You may set some cakes out on a plate. Check the tins for me, Sophie. These days it is hard for me to bend down.'

Sophie dropped to her knees, as if about to say her prayers, before a low cupboard. The doors stuck, so she had to yank the ridged plastic handle with both hands to get them to open. She opened three tins before she found a couple of lamingtons, surrounded by drifts of desiccated coconut, washed up on a square of greaseproof paper. It wasn't like Mrs P. Usually the tins were full of baking: jumblies and peppermint slices, Afghans and Belgian biscuits, and cake, always cake, as if at any moment Mrs P. might need to cater for a party.

Above her, Sophie heard the sound of the tea caddy opening, the clang of the spoon against the rim of the teapot, the gush of water onto the leaves making them release their sharp smell.

Mrs P. switched on an electric heater and the air filled with the smell of burning dust. As Sophie looked at the lamingtons, her stomach growled, the sound low and long and as full of intent as a guard dog inching towards an intruder.

'Go on, then, help yourself. Goodness me. You are a hungry, growing girl, aren't you? Are you eleven yet?'

Mrs P. always forgot. *I'm ten*, Sophie wanted to say, yet again, *ten*, but if she did that then Mrs P. would look up at the photograph on the mantelpiece, of the girl with long black plaits tied with ribbons at the ends. The photo was of Mrs P.'s daughter, Zosia, a silky ribbon of a name. The mantelpiece was crammed with photographs of Mrs P.'s family; dark-haired, dark-eyed, the men's shirts startlingly white, the women's blouses ruffled, and the women all with that same, slick hair, bunned at the neck's nape; they were Mrs P.'s family and all of them were dead. They smiled in the photographs, though, not knowing it.

'When is *your* birthday, Mrs P.?' Sophie pursed her lips to sip the tea. It was rude to ask people, especially old people, their age directly.

Mrs P. raised her eyebrows. 'I will be seventy tomorrow. Three score years and ten, the allotted span.'

'Will you have cake?' Sophie tightened her grip on the teacup.

'Cake? What cake, child?'

'Birthday cake.'

Mrs P. made the most wonderful chocolate cake, quite unlike the cakes anyone else made. It was gooey yet smooth, light yet substantial, bitter yet sweet. Outside, the drizzle had turned to a steady, soaking rain. A blackbird hopped up into the shelter of the yew tree, whose small dark leaves were sprinkled, at this time of year, with jelly-red berries.

'Cake,' Mrs P. said. 'Tomorrow.'

She seemed not to understand. Sophie feared her heart was not in her words. How could she change the subject, before Mrs P.'s eyes drifted up to the picture of Zosia? Looking into her cup, Sophie noticed a few tea leaves, which had escaped the strainer, floating beneath the milky swill.

'Will you tell my leaves, please?'

Mrs P.'s eyes focused and sought her out. With a naughty smile, she pushed the teapot towards Sophie.

'If you promise me you won't tell your mother, or these good Presbyterian neighbours of mine will run me out of town for being a witch.'

Sophie splashed more tea into her cup, drowning the pattern of forget-me-nots, then, after letting the leaves settle, carefully drained the liquid through her teeth. She pushed the cup towards Mrs P. who swirled the dregs and then upended the cup onto the saucer. More liquid slid out, like the brown juice that seeped from the bottom of the compost heap, as it did when that policeman came, most Saturday mornings, to dig bait worms out of it.

'Hmm,' Mrs P. peered into the cup, as if into a pale cave. 'Hmm,' she leaned back in her chair. 'I see, I see … cake. Lots of cake.'

Sophie's smile stretched her mouth so much it made her cheeks ache. 'Cake! What sort of cake?'

'Oh, it is big and brown and covered in chocolate.'

'Oh cake, cake, hurray for cake!' As Sophie stood up, her napkin flew from her lap to the floor.

Mrs P. opened her mouth and little laughs chugged out of it.

'You will enjoy eating it.'

'Yes. Yes, I will.'

'Then I will make one, just for you.'

'Thanks, Mrs P. Now … it's your turn.'

Mrs P. pursed her lips as if she were about to say, *Not today*, but then she poured some tea in her cup and repeated the ritual. Looking inside, she shook her head.

'What is it? What do you see?'

'I see that I am an old woman.'

Were those tears? Sophie scuttled round the table, nudging into Mrs P.'s side as a lamb pushes into its mother. Staring down into the mess of leaves, she began to pick out a picture of – what was it? Yes, that was it: the brick porch, the pile of firewood, a white streak of china that could have been a milk bottle standing sentry by the door.

Sighing, Mrs P. put down the cup. 'Perhaps we should do your hair.'

Red and curled, it was apparently just like her father's had been. From the dresser, Mrs P. pulled out a silver-backed brush and Sophie stared ahead, out into the world of rain, tears stinging her eyes as the brush snagged on tangles. As Mrs P. brushed, she hummed tunes which

sounded like strange lullabies under her breath – *la la lee,
la la lee* – and then began to plait, tugging and twisting
like a fiend and then, worst of all, bandaged the end of the
plaits in ribbons, as red as the yew-berries, which clashed
catastrophically with Sophie's hair.

A light flashed on from Sophie's house, casting a beam
of brightness across the grass. 'I'd better run. Mother'll
want me home for tea. Thanks, Mrs P.'

'It *is* late. I hadn't realised.' Mrs P. gave the bows at the
end of each plait a final tweak.

'I'll see you tomorrow, after school.' Mrs P.'s cheek felt
cold and almost wet, like snow that has begun to melt. 'I'll
make you a special card. Don't forget the cake.'

Speeding down the hallway, Sophie rattled out the
door and across the grass. The rain had almost spluttered
out. As Sophie opened the kitchen door, she smelt macaroni cheese.

'Yum,' she called, 'yum, yum, yum.'

Her mother placed a plate on the table. 'How was Mrs
P.?'

'She looked tired.' Sophie's fingers traced circles around
her eyes. 'It's her seventieth birthday tomorrow; she said
I could go back for cake after school. She's going to make
the super chocolatey one.'

'It would have been your father's birthday today.'
Sophie's mother said. 'Did you remember?'

At the mention of her father, a bubble of acid rose in
Sophie's throat. On the plate before her, the macaroni
writhed into maggots, the tomato sauce she'd squirted
over it to splatters of blood. Her Dad had been a soldier
somewhere called Korea. That word was hollow, the
big, white, empty space in the centre of a circle. After he
came back, he stopped shaving and slept during the day.
And then one day he woke up dead. Mrs P. sometimes
talked about another war, which meant she'd had to leave
Poland. The only things she'd brought with her were the

photographs of her family, *And,* she sometimes said, tapping the side of her head, *the things that live in here.*

After dinner – *Not hungry, Sophie? Too much afternoon tea at Mrs P.'s? You usually love your macaroni cheese* – followed by her mother's hand anxiously compressing her forehead, Sophie retreated to her room. She folded a clean, white sheet of paper in half then drew on it the number seventy made out of balloons. Her crayons were worn, scabby. She wasn't sure what else to draw. The cake? But her brown crayon was horrible, a bit yellowish like khaki, so that instead of looking like lovely silky chocolate, the cake in the picture came out the colour of horse manure.

On the way to school the next day, Sophie popped the card through Mrs P.'s letterbox. The porch looked the same as the day before: the neat wood pile, the web-filled boots, a fresh bottle of milk, pale as bone.

Because it was Mrs P.'s birthday, Sophie kept the red ribbons in her hair; at school, no one seemed to notice them, let alone tease her about them. As the day wore on, Sophie forgot about Mrs P. It was only on the way home, when they were passing the house and she saw the milk bottle still standing on the porch, that she remembered. Tugging her mother's hand, she said, 'We need to see Mrs P., remember. To say happy birthday.'

Her mother knocked then knocked again. 'It's Beverley Champion from next door. Are you all right, Mrs P.?' There was some kind of insistence in her mother's words, like the headmistress's voice on Anzac Day when she recited, *At the going down of the sun, and in the morning, we will remember them.*

Bored with waiting, Sophie wandered down the side path; after counting rooms in her head, she peered through one of the windows. Thick velvet curtains had been pulled across but there was a gap. As her eyes adjusted, she saw what looked like Mrs P.'s feet on the duvet. But why had she worn her shoes to bed?

Spooked as a rabbit, Sophie zigzagged back to the porch. Her mother's ear was pressed to the navy paint of the door. As Sophie grabbed her leg, her mother looked around and said, 'What? What is it?'

'She's asleep on the bed. She's wearing her shoes.'

Her mother pushed the door with both hands and it opened. 'Stay out here, Sophie. Mrs P.? Everything okay? Are you there?'

Sophie scuffed her toes through the dried leaves, which had gathered in little bundles on the porch, breaking them apart; seeing a movement in the gumboots, she peered in. A striped garden spider, bigger than a fifty pence piece, froze in the middle of its web. The milk waited; surely she should take it in and put it in the fridge, shouldn't she? Picking up the bottle, Sophie tiptoed inside. There was a print she liked in the hallway. Mrs P. said it was by a Dutch artist whose name Sophie could never remember. It showed a woman, half-turned away, who wore a blue dress and had what looked like blue feathers in her hair. She was picking something up – a letter? A bow? Or was she putting something away, folding a towel or something? Sophie was never sure. Sometimes it looked as though there might be a small, pleased smile on her face as if she'd found a loved object she thought she'd lost and other times, like today, it seemed as though the whole world made her sad. Sophie tiptoed on, past the open bedroom door. Her mother knelt by the bed, holding Mrs P.'s hand. Mrs P. had all her clothes on and was asleep on top of the bed, her skin as pale as milk.

Her mother looked around, 'I told you not to…'

'I was going to put the milk in the fridge.'

'Yes, I suppose we should.' Her mother let go of Mrs P.'s hand and, taking off her gloves, wiped her eyes.

Sophie's heart heaved, as if it were a little boat caught in a storm, riding wave after huge wave. Between her hands, the glass of the milk bottle seemed heavy, cold.

'I'm afraid Mrs P. has passed away. I'll need to call some people from next door.'

Mrs P. didn't have a telephone. *Why should I,* she always protested, *when I don't have anybody to ring?*

'Do you want to come with me?'

'I'll put the milk away.' It seemed wrong, somehow, to leave Mrs P. alone.

In the kitchen, baking things dried on the dish rack. As Sophie passed the oven, she felt a little residual heat ripple from it. Opening the fridge, she nestled the milk at the end of a long row of its fellows. In some of them, the milk had gone watery, and the sort of pale yellow colour you sometimes saw in the sky before the snow came. Not wanting to go back into the hallway, she slipped into the dining room.

In the middle of the table was a cake, just the sort Sophie loved, with thin wisps of chocolate, curled like wood shavings, on top of it. The photographs from the mantelpiece had been moved; they stood around the cake, a smiling crowd of well-wishers. Sophie's card sat among them. She knelt down by the table, looking at each of the smiling, expectant faces in turn. The photograph of Zosia, the girl with the ribbons, nestled close to its side. Sophie stared at the plaited hanks of hair, imagining them to be as dark and glossy as a blackbird's feathers. Moving the picture aside, Sophie's fingers slipped over the cake's sides, working until she had opened a flap, hinged like a door, in the icing and peeled it back. Burrowing with her fingers, she stuffed finger-loads into her mouth where it exploded sweetly, coating her teeth and tongue.

When she had made a long, rectangular cavity, Sophie tore the red ribbons from the end of her plaits and stuffed them inside before carefully smoothing the flap shut. To cover the wound, she pushed Zosia's photograph sideways, wiping away a brown fingerprint on the glass with her sleeve. Hearing floorboards creak under booted feet,

Sophie peeked into the hallway. A man stood there, the same policeman who came to dig worms from their compost heap. Her mother was with him.

'I've been trying to keep an eye on her. She was a lovely lady. I wish…'

'No one's going to sit in judgement. They don't insist on burying them down at the crossroads any more. Oh, Beverley. I'm sorry. I didn't mean to ... I'm so sorry, Beverley.'

As the policeman put his arm around her mother's shoulder, a crunching pain filled Sophie's stomach. She hated the way the policeman pulled the worms out of the darkness, imprisoning them into a jar so that he could later thread them on a hook. What did he mean about burying Mrs P. at the crossroads? Which crossroads? The whole town was flat, laid out on a grid. Sophie didn't remember seeing any graves on the street corners.

She walked out into the hallway and stood beside her mother. Outside, a rain shower swept over the houses, brief but intense: in its wake, water plipped from the gutters. They had to wait for some time before they saw the blue light of the ambulance flicker on the wet asphalt of the street.

'It's time to go home now. There's nothing more we can do.' But instead of moving her mother stayed still, her hand resting on Sophie's shoulder until the ambulance men carried Mrs P.'s body, covered by a night blue blanket, outside. The bottom of Mrs P.'s shoes still had the price label stuck on them. Then Sophie looked up, possibly for the last time, at the woman in the painting with blue feathers in her hair.

'Poor Mrs P.,' Sophie's mother said, sniffing.

'I'll come over home with you,' the worm policeman said, 'to make sure you're all right.'

'Run ahead, Sophie, and put the kettle on.' Her mother handed her the latchkey. 'Officer Welch will want a cup of tea.'

Sophie ran, holding her breath until her lungs screamed for air. In the kitchen, she pulled a pint of milk from the fridge and gulped some straight from the bottle; the milk seemed to cling to the chocolate in her mouth and wash it down until it was deep inside her. Soon, she would watch them slot Mrs P. into the brown earth, and spoon big crumbs of soil over her. Against the whiteness of the bottle, Sophie saw her nails were lined with chocolate. Putting them into her mouth, she sucked and nibbled them until every trace of cake was gone, wondering if anyone would notice the damage she'd done, both wishing and not wishing that she had eaten more.

Albatross

'I think we should sleep in the same bed tonight,' Fiona told Laura as they pulled up outside the cottage.

'Why on earth do you think that?'

Fiona shook her head so that her silver earrings jangled in the light. 'I've decided that we are just like Katherine Mansfield and Ida Baker. So you probably have repressed lesbian feelings for me.'

'What *are* you talking about?' They had been best friends for three years or so but lately Fiona's behaviour was increasingly bizarre. On the way down in the car, Fiona had told her she was on another diet, one where she'd eat nothing till teatime and then only consume one type of food – a baked potato, for example, or a tin of sweetcorn. Maybe that had something to do with it?

'Oh, never mind.' Fiona checked her lipstick in the mirror. 'We'll talk about it after.'

The keyhole was rusty. Fiona jiggled and jiggled the key until finally it turned.

'Shall we have a cup of tea?' Laura suggested.

'All you ever think about is food.'

'Food? I just thought, well, never mind.'

'We'll go for a long walk, and then we'll deserve a reward. That's what's wrong with you, Laura; all you ever do is eat, eat, eat.'

Fiona had always had a tendency to be abrupt but in the weeks since they'd finished secondary school, things had changed. Was it the influence of Fiona's boyfriend, Jake, or her new-found popularity? When Laura had first met her she'd been quiet, plain, studious.

'We'll sleep in here.' Fiona opened the door to a room with a double bed squeezed into a corner under a low ceiling. A small window gave a view of the bay, of sand and pines and lupins, bright as fireworks, dotted along the domain.

'I don't think…' Laura said, but Fiona walked away. Fiona's hands were always jittery now – was it the lack of food, or had she been taking drugs? It would explain her sudden lack of inhibition. Maybe Jake, who was two years older, had given them to her?

Laura put her holdall down in the living room. Inside she could see the baggy shapes of the clothes she'd stuffed in it. Fiona was right – Laura was overweight, unattractive at the age when what mattered more than anything was how you looked. At home, everything was falling apart and she lived, more or less, in a war zone. She had tried to tell Fiona, but Fiona didn't want to know.

The air inside the cottage was warm and yeasty with mould. Laura went outside and sat on the wooden steps. 'I will not cry,' she told herself, 'I will not cry.' Gorse pods exploded like gunshots in the hot dunes. In the sand hills behind her was a marae, and beyond that a penguin colony but at this moment, because of Fiona, none of it seemed to hold any magic.

'I forgot about the bikes.' When Fiona came out she had

reapplied her lipstick and put on a designer denim jacket. 'We can cycle to the headland.'

The cycles, old ten-speeds, were plaqued with rust. Laura's saddle creaked as they rode off the sand and onto the road. Fiona raced ahead, then, when she was far ahead of Laura, began to coast down the white road. At the shop Fiona stopped and bought drinks. Laura got off her bike and sat down in the shade of a pine.

Fiona squatted down next to her. 'Jake says I'm probably the re-incarnation of Katherine Mansfield. I'm one of those people that stand out as exceptional even when young. I've been reading her biography and I think Jake's right – don't you?'

'I like her stories but it was a sad life, wasn't it, really? Never quite finding the person she loved; getting sick, dying young...'

'Sad? No. She was a genius. She got away from New Zealand and had all those lovers. And then there was Ida, her so-called friend, who used to trail around after her. Katherine treated her like a slave.'

'I remember reading something about that.'

'And you know what? Katherine made Ida do her housework so she could spend her time writing. I bought a book of her stories with me. I'll read one to you later.'

What was the name of that story that Katherine Mansfield had written? It was about a family staying at a seaside place, not too dissimilar from this one. Laura loved the part where the little girl is talking to her grandmother. They're supposed to be having a siesta but the grandmother is knitting and sighing and the little girl asks her what she's thinking about. *Uncle William,* says the grandmother, *who has died,* and the little girl asks, *Does everybody have to die?*

'At The Bay,' Laura mumbled.

'What was that?' Fiona snapped, screwing the cap back on her bottle of Lucozade.

'Nothing; doesn't matter,' Laura shook her head. Katherine Mansfield might have been a bitch to Ida, but she was a good writer – no, not just *good*; she was a writer whose words resonated, like bells ringing through still, morning air.

They got back on their bikes. After passing through stone gateposts, they began to climb the hill. The road was lined, on the seaward side, with gun emplacements, built to protect the harbour from an attack (by the Russians, or was it the Japanese?) that had never come. Albatrosses nested on the very end of the headland, near the lighthouse. It was too steep to pedal. Laura got off her bike, wiped her face and started pushing. Ahead of her, Fiona wobbled then let her bike drop on the gravel. Teetering to the grass verge, she sat down.

'You know,' said Fiona when Laura came and settled next to her. 'I don't think I can make it. Anyway, it'll be dark soon. We'll want to get back to the cottage. I brought some wine.'

'Let's stop here a minute. Catch our breath.'

'You're unfit. It's all that extra weight.'

Laura plucked at a blade of grass, rolling it in her fingers. The things Fiona said no longer seemed like things a friend would say.

They looked down on Aramoana; the wetlands beyond it glinted like silver lace. The coast stretched away to the north, headland and inlet, beach and promontory, progressively fading until the land seemed to evaporate in the vicinity of Waianakarua. An albatross flew by, on wide, white wings, and hung for a moment on the wind, eyeing them. Laura caught her breath. The albatross's feathers were pure white, as if the Antarctic wind had plucked any colour from them – only a teeny bit of the feather ends was tipped with black.

Fiona squinted at it. 'You know Katherine used to call Ida "albatross".'

Laura sighed, and let the blade of grass drop from between her fingers. Fiona meant, of course, that an albatross was a curse, a wearisome burden, an encumbrance; she meant that there was something *wrong* with being an albatross; that the dynamic soaring that enabled them to cover great distances, the way they slope-soared off waves, robbing them of energy, stealing their wind, meant nothing; that Laura was a klepto-parasite, always trying to steal some vitality, some vividness from her. The albatross turned and skimmed away – it would fly for hundreds of miles, never tiring. Laura wanted to leap up, open her arms and soar, the updraft from the cliff buoying her, wings locked, suddenly light, until Fiona was far behind her, a puny stick insect trembling on a leaf. Laura smiled.

'What's so funny?' said Fiona. 'It's weird that you should think it's funny. That's what Jake says: you're weird, you're like a leech. He says I should just ping you off.' Fiona flicked a fingernail against the pad of her fingertip.

Laura got up, stretched her arms and got on her bicycle. The saddle, when she mounted it, made no protest. Without waiting, she took off down the road. There was a rhythm to cycling and she found it; using gravity, she got all the way back to the cottage without Fiona catching up with her.

The door was unlocked. Inside, it was as stuffy as it had been earlier. The book of Katherine Mansfield's stories lay on the table. Laura glanced through the pages, their edges age-yellowed. Here it was; the scene she was looking for in 'At The Bay'. The little girl is trying to get her grandmother to make a promise never to die. She starts to kiss her, and then the grandmother tickles the girl and they laugh and the grandmother says, *That's enough, my squirrel! That's enough, my wild pony…*

'That's enough,' said Laura, closing the book. She left it on the table, picked up her bag and got onto the bicycle.

The handful of things she would need for her journey weren't material; she could hold them quite easily in her mind. The rest was better left behind.

The Inlet

A knock at the door had woken him: Tim with the news that a girl, his girl, was missing. She was out there somewhere, in the tracts of farmland, on the coastal beaches, in the wild wetness of the estuary.

Cameron stood on the veranda of his farmhouse, peering down through light mist to the inlet. Tim waited beside him, pointing to a small figure moving across its surface. Low tide: the wide, shallow inlet little more than a basin of mud.

'John's got the sled. If she's out there, it's the only way to bring her back. We could lay boards, but that takes too much time. The tide'll be turning in an hour.'

Cameron found his gaze fixed on the man, labouring across the mud. John was the only one who still went out at low tide and dug for pipis by hand, as his father had done, and his father before him. Cameron's head throbbed. Now, when he needed to think, he couldn't and it was his own fault.

'At least it wasn't a cold night.' Tim shook his head. 'Where could she have gone?'

'What about Beth?'

'She's beside herself. Why don't you go down and…?' Tim bit his lip.

'If you see her, tell her I…' Cameron's throat was dry. Drawing a long breath in through his nose, he worked his tongue to moisten his mouth. 'Tell her…'

'It's all right. I will.'

Cameron pulled his Swanndri closer to his skin – the morning air was getting in, making him shiver – then stamped his boots on the boards. He couldn't wait any longer.

'I'll start checking the farm. Marama could have come up here, she sometimes does. I won't stop looking until I find her.'

A flat margin of land surrounded the inlet, a narrow gravel road running alongside the shore. Six scruffy wooden villas huddled there, half-hidden in scrubby manuka bushes, toitois and flax. Opposite them, three rickety boathouses hovered above the mud on rotting, weedy stilts.

'I'll head down now. Let Beth know we're all out looking.'

'Go. It's okay.' Cameron paced, his numb feet needling back to life.

'Sure?'

Cameron kept his eyes on the battered hide of his boots. Then, raising his head, said, 'Tell her…' but Tim had gone, running down the steep hillside, his feet leaving dark holes on the surface of the dewy grass.

As Cameron hurried up the steep, sheep-tracked hillside, a weak sun above him struggled to break through the mist. Six o'clock. How long had she been out here? How long had she been gone? As the wind picked up, he got a sniff of sea and turned towards the low humps of dunes at the inlet's mouth; beyond the dunes was a bone white beach. Usually the wind was a menace; it travelled across the Southern Ocean to make its first landfall here, a lateral wind, loaded with ice. It knifed through clothes, stripped the heat from you in seconds; it even somehow reached inside your teeth, and made them ring like bells. This morning, he was glad of it. It would blow the early morning mist away; it would clear his head faster than anything else; it would help him to find Marama.

Lights came on in the houses as Tim woke the sleepers. One light already burned. Why hadn't Beth told him sooner, why hadn't she noticed? He'd never asked her for anything, or expected anything from her. Neither of them had meant for it to happen, but it had happened. And the only good thing to have come out of any of it, the child called Marama, was lost.

'What should I do?' Six fifteen. He could feel his faults running through him, like cracks in an overused plate. What if she had got stuck on the mudflats; had fallen somewhere and twisted her ankle? Had she been crying out but no one had heard? It was overcast now, a fraction of drizzle; the lambs were calling their mothers. The dogs, smelling the morning, began to bark.

Cameron ran, slipping with every step on the wet hummocky grass, calling her name. He heard the sound of a tractor starting up, saw it out of the corner of his eye moving down the gravel road beside the inlet; for a moment he thought it must be old Watside rumbling along on his ancient red machine. But, of course, it couldn't be. Poor old boy had been on that sightseeing flight to Antarctica that had crashed into Mt Erebus. He'd been obsessed with the place, had sold most of his land up Tui Creek to raise the money for the flight, he'd even lived in one of the old creaking boatsheds that sat above the water of the inlet before he'd left. Watside used to stand on the beach for hours looking out at the Southern Ocean, rising up onto his tiptoes as if straining to see that place of ice; as if he believed he might glimpse it, if only he could stretch himself high enough above the waves' belly, the earth's curve.

At the boundary fence, where the paddock turned into a cliff and sheered down to the beach below, was a half-ruined cottage. Cameron ran inside but no; there was no sign of her. On the western wall was a stained-glass window, reminding him of the wooden church over the hill he had gone to when he was a child. He could never believe in what the hymns and the readings told him about a kind and loving God. His life on the farm seemed to be a struggle for survival, against weather and accident. Even now, he couldn't bring himself to call on God to save Marama. If God existed, it seemed to him, then he, or it, was something fierce and elemental and unquestionably inhuman, like the wind that came up from the ice, the relentless ocean, or even Antarctica itself, home of that wind: alone, inhospitable, extreme.

The south-facing window had blown out and, from it, Cameron could see the ceaseless shrugging of the sea. Light fell in dusty, shabby beams across the broken, dirty floor. The thought that he had been running from caught up with him: he was about to lose the thing most precious to him. It made him double up, like a blow in the stomach. He was a big man, and he knelt down awkwardly, as if it were hard for his body to bend itself, his eyes closing as he tried to think himself into her; wasn't she part of him, after all? And he saw her, paddling into the shallow waters of the inlet, her long, skinny legs making her look just like one of those wading birds they got on the shore; long brown hair, brown eyes, tanned skin, she blended into the estuarine pallet as seamlessly as a turnstone. He heard her squeals as her toes dug into the warm ooze for pipis, her triumph when she felt them and bent double, scrabbling them out with her hands. How old was she now? Six?

Seven?

He and Beth had only been together a few times. It had been one of those things that should never have happened, because she was already married. It hadn't taken him long to realise, after Marama was born. He had never stopped watching over her, turning from his work as he heard the school bus groan over the crest of the hill, watching her walk the dusty road, watching as she stopped to fossick on the shore.

Lurching up, Cameron started running towards the inlet. It was nothing more than instinct, nothing more than the thought that had gone through his mind as he knelt in the dust. A flare went up from out on the mud. The tide rushed back into the inlet, rapidly filling it – either John had found something, or he was in trouble himself. A group had gathered on the narrow shore of pebbles between the road and the mud. Cameron skidded as his feet hit the gravel, but instead of running towards them he made for the nearest boatshed, the one that had belonged to Watside. It was more derelict than the others, its stilts almost rotted through, home to hanging gardens of barnacles and weed. So many times he had seen Marama wading there and playing around the posts; he had worried for her, thinking the rotten shed might collapse on top of her.

As Cameron got close to the boatshed he could see the heel of a coloured sneaker almost buried in the mud. He shouted and waved his arms to the group on the shore, then swung himself up onto the bridge that connected the boatshed to the road, rotten pieces of wood breaking off beneath his hands. The door was locked but one kick opened it: none of them had gone anywhere near it since Watside had died, none of them except Marama. Inside, it was brighter than he expected: the walls were covered in maps of Antarctica, its white plains, its dry valleys, its islands, its mountains. She was there, curled up in the corner. She held her arm against her chest, her face pale, taut with pain, the freckles prominent against her skin.

'My arm, it hurts.'

'Hold on, girl.' Carefully, as if she were made of shell, Cameron lifted her. She must be dehydrated, in shock still, and pain. 'Did you fall, love? Hurt yourself?'

Marama nodded.

'You're safe now. I've got you.' As he stepped out onto the bridge, he shouted again; not a word, just a sound rose from the very centre of his chest. Marama flinched, and he wanted to stop, in case he was hurting her. Someone turned, their face a blur, and started to run towards him. The pebbles in front of him seemed to explode as a flock of godwits abandoned their camouflage and flung themselves into the air. He could see who it was now.

'Ambulance. Call an ambulance.'

Beth's legs gave way beneath her.

'She's all right; she's going to be all right.'

He carried Marama a few steps further then, kneeling on the dusty road, with a sure, tender gesture, placed his child back into the arms of her mother.

Learning To Be

was not always like this; once, there was more of me. Imagine this skeleton re-clothed, blackbird glossy, fleshy-plump. *She,* as I always think of the young me, was dissatisfaction incarnate, and look where *she* got me. We were, Murry and me, unable to become one whole being; despite our best efforts, we remained separate.

Was he the one? I expect so, yes; the love of one's life (and there must always somehow *be* one.) Was *she* not his love? People say so, but they do not look deeply enough. We were not what we seemed, as many are not; tugging and clawing, this way and that, sometimes miles apart, sometimes inches, tantalisingly close, on the cusp of ... what?

Were you not jealous of us? Did you imagine perfection, or did you see through our smokescreen, that bubbling pot of penury, misunderstanding, lust? Was he not, in the end, what he had planned all along to be: the great man of letters, living fat off my money with three more wives?

Was he not in the end, of the two of us, the more beautiful?

Were you not surprised? That it is my face, not his, which swims up from the dark. We were not the only ones who failed to learn the language of another; words stay on the page; people slide, slip and change.

Was *she* surprised at her fall from grace? *She* left on our wedding day, when he turned and, on his handkerchief, wiped our kiss off his lips.

Was he aware of what he did?

We were married at last, but there were no guests at our wedding breakfast, no photographs.

She was gone and I came back, my mother and my father, too, and Leslie and dear Granny, as they had come on the Quai des Fleurs, the river grey below Carco's window.

I was, after all, the long-searched-for cure.

The Lost of Syros

This morning, I sat in the chair that captures the earliest sunlight and opened the Saturday newspaper. Through the slightly open window, along with a puff of still cool April air, came the ecstatic shouts of kids released, like dogs from their leashes, onto the wide spaces of Hampstead Heath. I always put the travel section aside because I don't get the chance to go abroad much these days, but today one word caught my eye and, leafing past pages of last-minute deals, I came to a picture of the island.

There was Hermoupoli, crouching above its glittering, boat-littered bay, its elegant muddled buildings, paint faded to the soft pastel tones of sugared almonds, rising in jumbled confusion up the brown hillside, a Greek Orthodox church on one summit, a Catholic church on another. Twenty years ago, I had idled away three months there. Now there were grey hairs at my temples. I dropped the paper on the floor and moved my left hand to the empty space around my right wrist, pressing my fingers against my thumb until I formed a circle, enclosing it.

I had decided, almost at random, to have a week's stop-over in Syros on my way to London but after spending a couple of listless, jet-lagged days on the island, bored and restless, I had booked a ticket to travel to Mykonos on the lunchtime ferry. I was waiting at a café on the quay, my bags beside me, when a beaten-up black Peugeot pulled up and three people tumbled out of it.

'I'm Aris.' The tall, green-eyed man introduced himself first. 'This is Spiro and this is Magdalena.' Spiro was a lot older than Aris and the woman, who were in their twenties, like me. In profile, Aris's elongated face gave him the haughty look of an Assyrian king. 'May we join you in the shade?'

'I'm about to catch the ferry.'

It was already nosing its way into the harbour, conspicuous as a white whale amongst the tiny red and blue fishing boats jostling about their buoys, foghorn blasting although it was a clear day.

'What, you're leaving?' Aris threw up his hands. 'How long you been here?'

'Three days.'

'Where have you been?'

I told them.

'Let me see your ticket,' Aris said.

After I handed it to him, he inspected it for a moment and then tore it up.

'You're staying here. We'll show you around. If you still don't like it, I'll buy you another ticket to Mykonos in a few days.' As Aris enunciated the island's name his mouth curled, as if the word disgusted him.

The September wind, warm and muscular, blew the pieces of ticket off the table and carried them out to drown amongst the white, wavering buildings of the mirror city reflected on the harbour waters. I thought of yelling at Aris but, as the ticket was already torn up and now irreversibly soggy, it seemed a little late to worry. After a series of romantic and educational disasters, having barely scraped through my degree, feeling lost to myself as well as to my family, for the first time in my life I had no plan. I had wandered the white shores of the island blindly; I'd swum in the warm, weedy sea. I'd glanced down shaded pathways and into frantic cafés before moving swiftly past; I'd eaten meals of bread and cheese spread and oregano-flavoured crisps between the four walls of my whitewashed hotel room.

Aris offered me one of his cigarettes. Spiro lit one of his. Magdalena watched us, sometimes offering a comment in guttural Greek. Aris and Spiro spoke English but she didn't. From time to time she brushed dust from the knees of her jeans. Around her neck was a necklace made of knotted leather; she wore a Harley-Davidson tee shirt, and despite the heat, heavy boots.

Aris, noticing me studying her clothing, said, 'Magdalena likes motorbikes. She's Spiro's girlfriend for the summer while his wife is away.'

'Oh, I see.' Magdalena didn't look the type to be a married man's mistress but then, what did I know?

'There was an accident. She fell off the back of her boyfriend's bike. Look.' Spiro put his fingers under her chin and gently raised it to reveal a neck covered in white scar tissue. A wave-like pattern zigzagged around her jaw where, he said, the flaming petrol had burnt her. Spiro ran his finger over the curves. Aris ordered more coffee. No one said anything for a while.

'What happened to her boyfriend?'

Spiro asked her and then translated her answer. 'There was only one helmet. He made her wear it.' For a moment he rested his fingers lightly against his temple. 'He died.'

That night, Aris called for me at my hotel, and we went

to a bar to meet Spiro and Magdalena. They took me to a restaurant on the hillside above the port; built into an old archway, it once formed part of defensive wall built against the many waves of invasion the island had suffered by Phoenicians, Romans, Sicilians, Arabs, Ottomans and Venetians.

We ate fish, bread and salad, then grilled meat with lemon squeezed over it. We drank ouzo, cloudy with water, except for Magdalena who neither drank nor smoked. It took me some time to convince them that New Zealand was a real country and, even then, they were all adamant that it was part of Australia, which is about the worst insult a New Zealander (even a half-Australian one like me) can hear.

After a while I found it refreshed me: at home I had been labelled and tagged with a history I'd never shake off, but here my past, my country even, didn't exist. Being surrounded by a language I could neither speak nor understand was equally restful as if, after years in the desert, I'd found myself in a shade-filled garden by a pool of cool water, a place where I was expected to do nothing more than to listen and be still.

We met again the next day and went to the beach. In the sea, Magdalena and I had a handstand competition. She punched my shoulder quite hard, but with affection, when I won. Her hair was light brown, fine and wavy, and she had pale, freckled skin; at least I supposed they were freckles rather than splatter marks from the burning petrol. After swimming, when we stopped at a café for frappés and *tost,* Aris loaned some money from me to play a video game. Spiro watched him, clacking worry beads.

'You like Aris? ' he asked me.

I nodded. I did like Aris.

'You going to stay here long?'

'For a little while. Then I'm going to London.'

'I've been to London. I didn't like it. It's very cold.'

Spiro's face was smooth, despite his age, which I guessed was around forty, almost double mine. His hair, parted in the middle, waved down to his shoulders, Jesus-style. He wore shirts, never tee shirts: along with decent shorts and leather sandals, his dress gave him an air of above average sophistication. There was a sense of deep relaxation about him, and I wondered if he did a lot of yoga, or took drugs. His features were generous, widely spaced, rounded and soft, reminding me of the faces of home. Magdalena rubbed his arm and growled something at him.

'What's up?'

'She's jealous. Wants to know what I'm talking to you about. She thinks I'm chatting you up.'

Magdalena, tired of us talking again, said, 'Eh, Spiro,' and when he turned she punched him gently on the side of the head.

I smiled at Magdalena to reassure her. But there *was* something appealing about Spiro, perhaps his palpable calmness, so different from the frenzied air of so many of my friends. Behind us, Aris swore and whacked the pinball machine with the side of his hand. Then he lifted the front legs of the machine off the ground and let it crash back down on the wooden floor.

Aris had a job lugging boxes around in the mornings. During the day I walked through the town, along the lines of shadow, stopping occasionally for frappés. In the evening, I met Aris. There was a bar on the waterfront near the commercial end of town that sold the best grilled octopus, bathed in lemon vinegar, as a bar snack; often we'd run into Spiro and Magdalena. We sipped aniseedy ouzo, before biting into chunks of octopus, sweet and lemony and smoky from the grill. Bottles of vinegar and a jar of toothpicks held the tablecloth down against a wind still rough enough to make the boats in the harbour knock together like wooden chimes and waves slap over the concrete dock. One night we went to a restaurant in a boatyard, a shack huddled beneath the bare ribs of a ship's skeleton.

'Eat more,' they urged me. 'You drink too much and don't eat enough. Why?'

It was hard to answer questions like that, almost as hard as it was to explain why I'd laughed when Aris told me his full name was Aristotle. Finally I said, 'Where I come from, everybody does. Everyone I know. It's just one of those things.' The food was good and, as I ate, I could feel the past working itself out of me, sour as the local wine upon my tongue.

After dinner, we went to a bar away from the bright lights of the Maiouli Square. Once we were inside the owner, a school friend of Aris's, turned down the lights and locked the doors. A group of men gathered around the pool table and started throwing dice. Spiro waited, sitting in the shadows with Magdalena and me, before joining them. The men he was playing against were much younger than him, and had had far more to drink. Some were still in their teens.

Aris, who had started playing at once, lost his money quickly and joined us at the table. He sulked for a little while until I bought him another ouzo.

'It's illegal, you know, this dice game.' Aris nodded toward the pool table, where the boys' faces appeared out of deep shadows like the faces in Velasquez's paintings of *bogedones*. 'Except on New Year's Eve. Then everybody plays.' Looking in Spiro's direction, Aris narrowed his eyes. 'Spiro's a gambler. All winter he plays to earn enough money to lie on the beach all summer. But it doesn't really matter because he's got a rich wife. She's Swiss or French or something; works for the UN. She comes here for a few weeks a year but the rest of the time he can do what he likes.'

Magdalena watched as Spiro's face caught the light

from the low bulb over the pool table; again and again, he threw the dice and, again and again, scooped up the notes and coins laid out on the table's edge.

'What will happen to Magdalena when Spiro's wife comes?'

'Magdalena will have to go back to Athens. None of us see Spiro when his wife is here; then, he doesn't know any of his friends. If you see him on the street he'll look right through you, walk straight past you, as if you were a ghost.'

On a different beach, on the far side of the island, half-hidden behind a scrubby band of tamarisks, was a ruined pink villa; in its spacious bedraggled grounds a pine tree grew in an abandoned swimming pool. It was on that beach that I got into the habit of writing my name on the sand in shells, and, increasingly often, the names of the others. Each time we returned to the beach I'd search for the marks I'd made, only to find they had washed away. Once Spiro came up to me and placed his arm around my neck. He opened his mouth as if he were about to speak but no words came, only the pressure of his hand closing as he squeezed my shoulder.

After I had spent some weeks on the island, Spiro invited us to visit him and Magdalena at home.

'Strange,' Aris muttered, 'he doesn't usually invite people to his house.' He looked at me intently. He was always suspicious of the motives of all the other men on the island and, increasingly, he found fault with the things I said or did, or didn't say or didn't do.

Spiro's house stood on a promontory, on a rugged stretch of coast which faced out over the sea. Below the house was a private pebble beach and cove where the water was turquoise and purple. The design of the house was simple: one storey; built of sandstone; a wooden veranda curved around its west and south sides. When we arrived, Spiro said Magdalena was asleep. Spiro was preparing pigeon for dinner and the sweet and savoury smell of softened onions, tomatoes and potatoes filled the simply furnished, whitewashed rooms.

When Spiro was finished in the kitchen, we sat together on the veranda in the late sunlight, sipping ouzo and nibbling pistachio nuts. Carved pieces of sandstone, about two feet square, were propped against the walls: on them were carvings, images of moons, stars, suns, dolphins, flowers. Spiro was a sculptor as well as a gambler; the plaques he carved were to mark the place on the roadside where, after an accident, someone's life had ended: often, like Magdalena's boyfriend, they were young men who had ridden their motorbikes too fast on the island's winding gravel roads. I had noticed these memorials to the lost of Syros on dusty verges; sometimes they had been worn away by rain and sun, the patterns on them faded, until only the stone marker, pale and simple, remained.

We watched the sun go down into the dark sea, and as Spiro spoke of sailing to Rhodes in November to gamble in the casino, I remembered the day on the beach, the touch of his hand on my shoulder. Was this the place I had been looking for? Why hadn't I realised how I felt about him before? Was it seeing his house that had done it? His purple and turquoise bay? Or was it the carvings, standing patiently in the dusk, waiting for the next lost boy to claim one of them? When he noticed I wasn't speaking to him as much as usual, Spiro said, 'Is anything wrong?'

'It's nothing. I'm homesick, that's all.'

'But where is your home now?'

I was about to reply that I no longer knew when Magdalena came outside to join us, punching us all on the arm in her usual fashion.

'I've been teaching Magdalena to cook and now she's got quite good. It's a shame she has to leave.' Spiro turned to her, pulling her so she rested on the arm of his chair.

'Why does she have to leave?'

'My wife's coming home. So Magdalena will have to go back to Athens.'

They started talking in Greek. Spiro was smiling. Magdalena was smiling. Why was she smiling? Was I the only one who wanted to cry?

Aris laughed. 'She doesn't want to go. She's fallen in love with Spiro.'

We ate the potatoes and pigeon ('watch out for shot') and then, because it was October, Spiro lit the fire.

The next afternoon we met on the beach by the ruined villa. The sand was littered with small, dead fish amongst which a yowling kitten scavenged. Magdalena grabbed the kitten and saying, 'Eh, Spiro,' tried to get his attention first by pretending to drown it, and then by throwing it up into a tree.

'Ignore her,' Aris said.

But I was trying to ignore Spiro because, each time I looked at him, I had the feeling that he was the one I should be with. As Aris and Spiro walked ahead, discussing something, I walked behind with Magdalena. Though we could say nothing more to each other than 'Hello' and 'How are you?' she talked away to me in Greek and, from time to time, gave me a friendly punch on the arm. Spiro had bought her a new tee shirt, with a Triumph motorcycle logo on it, the sort Bob Dylan wore on the record cover of *Highway 61 Revisited*. As we left, Spiro explained that Magdalena would leave for Athens the next day.

Aris had got a new job planting telephone poles on the other side of the island. When he got home at lunchtime, exhausted by work and increasingly irritable, he wanted to sleep. Perhaps it was the news that Magdalena was going that prompted me, but I decided it was time for me to leave as well. I wanted to sneak off, so there wouldn't be a fuss, but in such a small place it was difficult to go anywhere without *someone* knowing. Everyone seemed to be related to each other; in moments of paranoia, I felt as though they were keeping an eye on me for Aris and reporting my movements back to him.

The next morning, after Aris had left for work, I set off for town to find out about the winter ferry schedule. There were sailings at 2.30pm, Tuesdays and Thursdays. Today was Tuesday. Perhaps I could make the Thursday ferry? After making a note of the price and dates, I was about to go to the bank to withdraw some money when I heard someone hail me.

Magdalena sat at the table of our favourite café, a glass of ouzo and a plate of octopus in front of her. When I saw her waving and smiling at me, tears crowded my eyes. She stood and hugged me, slapping me on the back. Motioning me to sit, she yelled for the barman. It took me about ten minutes to realise she was drunk. Across the road, people, buses, cars, crates and lorries were trundling into the maw of the Tuesday ferry. Magdalena was talking to me; I had no idea what she was saying only that, like me, she seemed on the edge of tears. We smashed our glasses together and drank as the ferry slipped its moorings and pulled away, hooting loud enough to rouse the ghosts of the dead boys sleeping beneath their plaques on the island roadsides.

Two ouzos later, a black Peugeot pulled up in front of the café. Spiro jumped out and ran up to our table, his voice raised to a shout, his words and gestures rapid. He slapped Magdalena on the cheek, knocking her head to the side so that the wrong, tender silver of her scarred neck showed. She laughed and, closing her eyes, braced herself for another impact of his hand, a slight smile playing around her lips. A light, white and blinding, poured through me and, slamming my drink down so hard the table wobbled, I grabbed Spiro's arm. 'Don't you dare touch her again! Leave her alone!'

'What are you doing here? Did she ask you to meet her?'

'Of course not! We don't speak the same language so how do you suppose we would arrange to meet?'

'Okay, okay.' After he had shaken off my hand, Spiro kicked the table. The barman, who had come to the doorway, wiped his hands slowly on a tea towel. After a moment or two, Spiro slumped onto a chair.

I glared at him, as if my eyes could burn right through him. Magdalena, no longer smiling, began to sob. Spiro called for more drinks and the barman, raising his shoulders in a shrug, his face weary, trudged back inside. Magdalena pressed her face against Spiro's chest and rubbed it back and forth, back and forth, until her tears soaked through his shirt. Spiro sipped his drink and then, raising his voice again, said, 'What am I going to do? My wife's arriving tomorrow. Magdalena can't stay with me anymore. She has to go back to Athens.'

'Why won't she go?'

'She's in love with me. She doesn't want to leave me.' He stroked her pretty brown hair.

'*You* made her love you and now you're throwing her away.'

'She knew what my situation was. She always knew this time would come.'

I picked up my drink and, closing my eyes, felt the ouzo slip down my throat, cool and soft as Spiro's hand had felt, that day on the beach, on my bare shoulder. When I opened them, Magdalena was talking to Spiro in a low voice.

'Magdalena says you are her friend. She says that you are nice and kind to her. All the other women look down on her but not you. She says you're the best friend she's ever had.'

From her wrist, Magdalena removed a bracelet, two thin black leather straps tied to either side of a silver plaque; the outlines of flowers and stars, a sun and a moon, had been cut out of the metal, as though it were a stencil. Leaning over, she fastened the ties around my wrist then punched me tenderly on the arm.

'*Efaristo poli.*'

'I better take Magdalena home,' Spiro said. 'She's very drunk.'

After he took her to the car, I sat in the bar a while longer and then I walked up the hill to my hotel.

I don't know how Magdalena got back to Athens. Spiro's wife arrived and, as Aris predicted, Spiro forgot about us. I did catch a glimpse of them once, driving through town in the black Peugeot. Spiro's wife had long blond hair; her eyes were hidden behind dark glasses. When I asked Aris what she was like all he would say was that she was rich and old, 'much older than Spiro.'

Aris and I came to an impasse. After what happened between Spiro and Magdalena in the café I no longer had any stomach for scenes. Aris asked me to try and extend my visa. When he talked about us getting married, all I could think of was the ruined pink villa by the beach, of the sand littered with dead fish. We went to ask about my visa, eventually ending up in the headquarters of the Security Police. In two weeks' time, when the stamp in my passport expired, I would need to leave, not just the island, but also the country. It put an end to our arguments, at least.

A week later, Aris said he had seen Spiro in town. Spiro's wife had left; they had arranged to meet that afternoon; that day was my twenty-second birthday. Behind the beach, the pink villa seemed, if anything, a little more dilapidated, the pine tree in the swimming pool evidence of a kind, like those luckless cities abandoned by their former inhabitants, surrounded by jungle and, except in vague story or memory, lost. On the shore, as always, I looked for the names I'd written on the sand. Only Magdalena's was still legible; the waves had washed mine, Spiro's and Aris's away.

Further down the beach, some men were struggling to launch a boat. Aris went over to help them. For the first and last time, Spiro and I were alone.

'You know he's no good, don't you?' Spiro said.

'Yes, I do.'

'You're too soft. You should say what you want.' He raised his shoulders and shrugged. 'You should get rid of him; he'll never amount to anything.'

I nodded. 'I know. I'm leaving in a couple of days.'

Spiro looked away from me, out towards the sea. 'Magdalena is coming back next week. She'll be sorry to miss you.'

'Tell her I said goodbye.'

Spiro said, 'You know…'

Aris came running back across the beach. Spiro got up and walked away from me. Aris pushed me, hard, saying, 'Did he ask you to go and live with him? I knew he would. He's always liked you.'

'Leave me alone. Don't touch me.' I saw Spiro's hand striking Magdalena's face, the white, scarred skin of her neck; raising my hand to my aching throat, I held it there.

In the final days, I walked through the old town, past the tiny whitewashed houses where the people still used donkeys to carry their groceries and firewood up the cobbled streets. I went into the cathedral to gaze at the votive offerings to saints dangling from every surface, as dark-eyed icons looked serenely on. I went to another church, out on a headland, where Aris's mother had told me the hills, bare as naked limbs after the summer, were covered with wildflowers at Easter. I deposited my final load of rubbish in the bin on the corner of the road, home to several families of rumbling, scavenging feral cats with odd-coloured eyes. I scuffed down to town, past the soldier boys with rifles guarding the barracks who always called out, 'Hey, blondie, give me a kiss or I'll shoot you.'

I passed the boatyard, and the café where I'd last seen Magdalena, and the bar where the late night dice game had been played, on and up through the old defensive wall, past the restaurant where we'd eaten together the first night I'd met them. I paused a moment at the café where I'd waited so many weeks ago for the ferry, and Aris had torn up my ticket. I may have cried a little. I don't know whether or not I was hoping to see Spiro again but our paths didn't cross.

When the day came for me to catch the ferry, Aris drove me into town and left me on the dock with my backpack, saying he was too upset to watch me leave. Standing there, I noticed that the wind had dropped; for the first time since I'd arrived, the water was as still and silver-grey as steel. On board, I found a seat and huddled down into my coat against the cold. It started to rain. As the ferry pulled away from the dock, I looked at the island for the last time and noticed a black car, squat as a beetle, pulled up by the side of the road. Squinting through the smudged pane streaked with raindrops I even thought I could see someone in it, watching me depart.

I wore the bracelet Magdalena gave me tied around my wrist, never once taking it off, even when I bathed or showered. I settled in London and got a job and told my-self that next summer I would go back to the island and see them again. It was December; London was dull and cold and grey; as time went on, the crystal light of the is-lands seemed to fade and, without my noticing, the thin leather which held the bracelet to my wrist must have worn through because one day I looked down to find that it had gone.

Notes and Acknowledgements

I would like to thank my husband, Adam, and my daughters, Iris and Lauren, for their constant love, support and encouragement. Thanks also to Rupert Wallis, Tam Ward, Sue Jackson and Nancy Kinnison for their valuable thoughts and comments on these stories over the five years during which they were written. My gratitude is due to competition judges Jane Gardam, Jacob Ross, Vanessa Gebbie, Ellen Phethean and Kathleen Kenny, as well as to Sheila Wakefield and the editors who have accepted my stories for publication.

Many thanks, also, to Maria C. McCarthy and Bob Carling at Cultured Llama for finding room for me in their stable.

'The Pledge' was first published by *Friction Magazine,* Issue One, 2010. It won The Society of Authors' Tom-Gallon Award 2011.

'The Glasshouse Mountains' was first published in *The Parabola Project,* Volume 1, Issue 2: Quickening (Telltales Publications, 2011). It won the Society of Women Writers and Journalists' Theodora Roscoe/Vera Brittain Cup Short Story Award 2011.

'Katherine And The Lighthouse' was first published by *bloc-online,* 2010. Second publication was in *The Parabola Project,* Volume 1, Issue 1: Origins (Telltales Publications, 2010). It was runner-up in the bloc-online competition, judged by Simon van Booy. After moving to Falmouth, Cornwall, I discovered that Katherine Mansfield and John Middleton Murry (known as Jack) had lived for a time in the nearby village of Mylor. During this time, they were visited by Fred Goodyear, a poet who was in love with Katherine. In her letters, Katherine mentions that she, Fred and Jack had a picnic at a beach near the lighthouse at St Anthony's Head.

'The Inlet' was first published online by Meridian Writing, 2010.

'Albatross' was first published in print by *The Yellow Room,* Issue Six, 2011.

'Kangaroos' was first published online on the webzine *Ink, Sweat and Tears,* 2011.

'Bright, Fine Gold' was first published online in *Spilling Ink Review,* Issue 7, 2011. (1) is a quote taken from a *New Scientist* article by Jeff Hecht, 7 September 1991 (Issue 1785).

'Painting Katherine' was first published in print by *The Frogmore Papers 81,* March 2013. In 1918, to recover from a bout of pleurisy, Katherine Mansfield returned to Cornwall and stayed in The Headland Hotel in Looe. She was looked after by her friend, the American painter Anne Estelle Rice, who painted a luminous portrait of her (now in the collection of Te Papa, the National Gallery of New Zealand).

'Learning To Be' was first published online by the webzine *Ink, Sweat and Tears,* 28 June, 2013. Before she died, on the last page of her notebook, Katherine Mansfield was conjugating the past tense of the verb 'to be' in Russian.

'A Walk In The Forest' was first published online by *Meniscus Journal*, The Association of Australian Writing Programmes, University of Canberra, September 2013.

'Transport' was first published in print in Issue 28 of *Dream Catcher* magazine, Spring 2014.

Cultured Llama Publishing
Poems | Stories | Curious Things

Cultured Llama was born in a converted stable. This creature of humble birth drank greedily from the creative source of the poets, writers, artists and musicians that visited, and soon the llama fulfilled the destiny of its given name.

Cultured Llama is a publishing house, a multi-arts events promoter and a fundraiser for charity. It aspires to quality from the first creative thought through to the finished product.

www.culturedllama.co.uk

Also published by Cultured Llama

Poetry

strange fruits by Maria C. McCarthy
Paperback; 72pp; 203×127mm; 978-0-9568921-0-2; July 2011

A Radiance by Bethany W. Pope
Paperback; 72pp; 203×127mm; 978-0-9568921-3-3; June 2012

The Strangest Thankyou by Richard Thomas
Paperback; 98pp; 203×127mm; 978-0-9568921-5-7; November 2012

Unauthorised Person by Philip Kane
Paperback; 74pp; 203×127mm; 978-0-9568921-4-0; November 2012

The Night My Sister Went to Hollywood by Hilda Sheehan
Paperback; 82pp; 203×127mm; 978-0-9568921-8-8; March 2013

Notes from a Bright Field by Rose Cook
Paperback; 104pp; 203×127mm; 978-0-9568921-9-5; July 2013

Sounds of the Real World by Gordon Meade
Paperback; 104pp; 203×127mm; 978-0-9926485-0-3; August 2013

Digging Up Paradise: Potatoes, People and Poetry in the Garden of England by Sarah Salway
Paperback; 164pp; 203×203mm; 978-0-9926485-6-5; June 2014

The Fire in Me Now by Michael Curtis
Paperback; 90pp; 203×127mm; 978-0-9926485-4-1; August 2014

Short of Breath by Vivien Jones
Paperback; 102pp; 203×127mm; 978-0-9926485-5-8; October 2014

Cold Light of Morning by Julian Colton
Paperback; 90pp; 203×127mm; 978-0-9926485-7-2; March 2015

Zygote Poems by Richard Thomas
Paperback; 62pp; 178×127mm; 978-0-9932119-5-9; June 2015

Automatic Writing by John Brewster
Paperback; 92pp; 203×127mm; 978-0-9926485-8-9; June 2015

Short stories

Canterbury Tales on a Cockcrow Morning by Maggie Harris
Paperback; 138pp; 203×127mm; 978-0-9568921-6-4; September 2012

As Long as it Takes by Maria C. McCarthy
Paperback; 168pp; 203×127mm; 978-0-9926485-1-0; February 2014

In Margate by Lunchtime by Maggie Harris
Paperback; 204pp; 203×127mm; 978-0-9926485-3-4; February 2015

Anthologies: poetry and short stories

Unexplored Territory edited by Maria C. McCarthy
Paperback; 112pp; 203×127mm; 978-0-9568921-7-1; November 2012

Non-fiction

Digging Up Paradise: Potatoes, People and Poetry in the Garden of England by Sarah Salway
Paperback; 164pp; 203×203mm; 978-0-9926485-6-5; June 2014

Punk Rock People Management: A No-Nonsense Guide to Hiring, Inspiring and Firing Staff by Peter Cook
Paperback; 40pp; 210×148mm; 978-0-9932119-0-4; February 2015

Do it Yourself: A History of Music in Medway by Stephen H. Morris
Paperback; 504pp; 229×152mm; 978-0-9926485-2-7; April 2015

The Music of Business: Business Excellence Fused with Music NEW EDITION by Peter Cook
Paperback; 318pp; 210×148mm; 978-0-9932119-1-1; May 2015